The characters and
Any similarities to real persons, living or dead, is
coincidental and not intended by the author.

PRAISE FOR
TYLER JONES

"Jones draws readers into this cosmic horror story as irresistibly as the mysterious undertow that pulls the protagonists "deeper and deeper into the dark" of the ocean."

- Publishers Weekly

"Gripping, visceral, and supremely unpredictable. It's tempting to try to describe the experience of *Heavy Oceans* as, like, *The Langoliers* meets *Black Tide* with a dash of Gabino Iglesias or S.A. Cosby, but the crystal-clear prose and the deft character work are pure Tyler Jones."

-Nat Cassidy, author of *Mary: An Awakening of Terror* and *Nestlings*

"Tyler Jones will crush you with the weight of these stories."

-Sadie "Mother Horror" Hartmann, author of *101 Horror Books to Read Before You're Murdered*

"Tyler Jones' stories are a manifesto for how horror can move, disturb, amuse, and devastate."

-Esquire Magazine on *Burn The Plans* (one of Esquire's Best Horror Books of 2022)

BOOKS BY
TYLER JONES

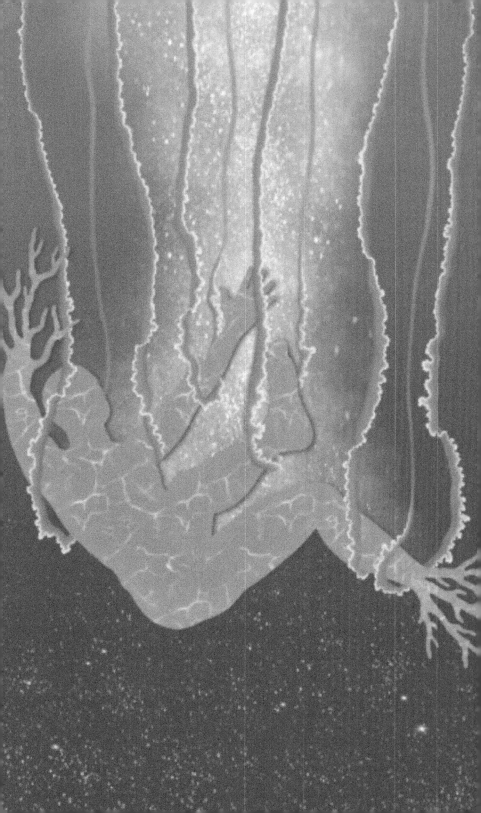

HEAVY OCEANS

TYLER JONES

DARKLIT
PRESS

CONTENT WARNING

The story that follows may contain graphic violence and gore.

Please go to the very back of the book for more detailed content warnings.

Beware of spoilers.

To Jim Wright
for showing me what integrity means,
for teaching me how to "hold fast"
for leading by example.

"There's an annihilation reaction… a hundred percent conversion of matter to energy… Gravity distorts time and space. And since you're distorting time, all this takes place in between moments of time."

- *Bob Lazar*

PROLOGUE

Jamie Fletcher woke to the sound of the top bunk creaking. He opened his eyes. The moon hung bright against an ink black sky. Mom had forgotten to say goodnight and close the curtains, so he saw straight out the window.

Normally, the moon wasn't so bright, but ever since Dad stormed outside with his .357 a few months earlier and shot out the streetlight (said it kept him awake), that part of the street was so dark you couldn't even see the sidewalk.

Dust particles floated through streaks of blue light as Eric's silhouette came climbing down the ladder, and the whole bed swayed a little with his weight.

When they first moved in, Jamie had wanted the top bunk, but Eric got to pick since he was two years older.

He knew better than to say or do anything that might startle his brother. It had been a couple months since his brother last sleepwalked, but Jamie remembered what Mom told him.

Follow him, make sure he doesn't do anything stupid or get himself hurt. If you can, guide him back to bed. Gently, though.

Eric's bare feet hit the floor, and for one brief moment Jamie saw his brother's face. His eyes stared, wide open, refusing to blink - stark against his skin -so pale in that moonlight - like he was dead.

Eric turned his head and looked at Jamie, sitting up, huddled in his blanket, and Jamie hated the feeling of being looked at but not seen. His heart rate jumped and he suddenly jolted from still half-asleep to fully awake.

Jamie told his friend at school about Eric's sleepwalking. Explained it like there was another person inside his brother, one who only came out at night, and wanted to do things that Awake Eric would never do. Like, make a piece of toast with Mom's marmalade. Eric didn't like marmalade. He always had strawberry jam on his toast.

Sleep Eric once arranged all the shoes by the front door in pairs, from biggest to smallest. Dad's left behind shoes, his own, Mom's, and Jamie's.

Sleep Eric sat at the dining room table and put together a 500-piece puzzle of the Giza Pyramids. And he did it fast.

Awake Eric hated puzzles.

Sleep Eric made an entire beef casserole with mashed potatoes one night. Stood cooking in the kitchen, stirring sauce, peeling potatoes.

Awake Eric had never cooked a meal in his life.

Once, Sleep Eric took Dad's rifle out of the hallway closet and stood in the living room, holding it like a soldier at attention, waiting for orders. Eventually, he put the gun back, but Jamie spent the next several weeks checking the rifle before bed to make sure it was unloaded. Like it would have mattered. If Sleep Eric could make a full dinner, he'd have no trouble finding bullets and loading the gun.

Jamie told his friend it was like watching a zombie if zombies weren't mean. Sleep Eric controlled the hands and feet, controlled the head, used the eyes, but he couldn't seem to make the mouth work. Sleep Eric never spoke. Three of those nights he grabbed a pencil and made weird pictures that weren't really pictures. Just hundreds of dots scribbled onto the paper in a random pattern. Some of the dots were bigger than others, but Jamie never could make sense of them, and of course, in the morning, Awake Eric would have no memory of what he'd done.

Sleep Eric only appeared every few weeks, so it took almost two months for Jamie to realize that every picture contained the same number of black dots, in exactly the same pattern.

He asked Awake Eric what the pictures meant, and his brother just shrugged and said, "I have no idea."

Eric always got sick after a night of sleepwalking. The very next day he'd spike a fever and be laid up in bed, sweating, muttering things that didn't make sense. He'd rub at a spot on his neck and whisper in a hoarse voice that it was sore. That it ached. Jamie slept on the couch on those nights, because he couldn't get any rest the way his brother thrashed around. The sickness usually only lasted a day or two and Eric would be back to his normal self. Only his "normal" changed after he began sleepwalking.

And when did it start?

It took Jamie a while to make the connection, and it happened by accident. He started keeping track of his brother's sleeping episodes up until they disappeared when Eric was sixteen. Jamie drew a little plus sign in the corner of the day. In his journal, which he hid under his pillow, he would write down the specifics of what Eric did, trying to look for a pattern, or a clue as to why he would undertake so many unusual tasks. And when Jamie looked back at the calendar, he saw another notation he made on the day of Eric's first sleepwalking episode.

"DG"

Dad Gone

Their father got into a screaming match with Mom. A bad one. The worst Jamie had seen. He knew it was bad because they were both screaming louder than the TV in the living room where the boys sat. Jamie heard every word coming from upstairs. And there was the heavy wood on wood sound of dresser drawers crashing open and slamming shut. One drawer ended up broken. Then the closet door, same thing. Even Dad's footsteps were so much harder than they needed to be. Like he was trying to bust a hole through the floor with each step.

This wasn't the first time Dad had left, but it felt different because he'd never packed anything before. Like, maybe he actually meant it this time.

When he came downstairs, dragging a suitcase that clunked against each step, he walked past the living room, then stopped, all out of breath, and said,

"You boys keep an eye on her. Make sure she don't burn down the place." When he reached the front door, he walked outside and said, "I'll be seeing ya."

The door slammed shut and a few seconds later Jamie heard the familiar growl of Dad's truck. He watched through the window as the taillights faded down the street, like two shrinking red eyes.

That night, Sleep Eric made his first appearance.

Jamie followed his brother downstairs, trailing his fingertips along the wall, feeling the frayed edges of a hole in the drywall the size and shape of Mom's head from when she tried to crawl away from Dad during a fight, up the steps on all fours like a dog.

Jamie wondered why Eric wouldn't respond to him whispering his name, whispering, "What are you doing?"

Eventually, the boys learned how to patch the drywall and erase the damage Dad had made with their bodies—heads, elbows, knees—hiding the holes in the walls that bled white powder.

Sleep Eric made his way through the kitchen to the living room. The couch and chairs were black silhouettes against black. Jamie cracked his shin against the edge of the coffee table and stifled a curse. He couldn't understand how Eric didn't bump into things. He brushed past countertops and furniture like he could see in the dark.

And Eric's walk, it wasn't a shuffle, and it wasn't uncertain. He moved with confidence from one room to the other, as if he woke up with a specific purpose and he couldn't see or hear anything unrelated.

The chain latch on the front door clicked aside and Sleep Eric shuffled out of the house into the cold night air. Barefoot. Jamie stopped to slip on a pair of shoes then hurried after his brother.

Whatever tasks those deep parts of Eric's brain thought he needed to do, they were always inside the house. He'd never ventured outside before, and even though Jamie wasn't worried about him falling into a ditch, he was desperately afraid a car would come tearing down the street and slam into his brother, send him sailing over the hood to land on the asphalt in a tangle of broken limbs.

As Eric left the front yard and walked into the street, Jamie looked both ways for him. A few cars were parked along the curb, but no headlights shone in either direction.

The streetlight Dad shot out was directly across from their house, and the light used to shine right into the master bedroom window. Their house was wrapped in darkness. The closest streetlight was two blocks away, a distant white glow.

Sleep Eric moved with purpose, toward a destination known only to him. Jamie turned to close the front door so it wouldn't bang into the wall and wake Mom, when he felt heat on his back. He turned around, heart thudding against his ribs as light flooded the front yard, revealing all the dead patches of grass where neighborhood dogs had pissed over the years.

Something glittered beneath the streetlight. Shards of glass from when Dad shot the light. Glass he never cleaned up. Sleep Eric was walking straight toward the light pole and Jamie yelled for him to stop. Yelled that his feet would get all cut up.

Eric stopped just beneath the broken streetlight. Only, it wasn't broken anymore. A brilliant beam of light shone down on him, making every hair on his head appear to glow. With his eyes open, he looked straight up into the light.

Jamie's legs finally came unglued, and he started running, waving his arms and yelling Eric's name. A sound came from the sky, or maybe it was more a feeling than a sound—a deep, bass-like thump in his chest that kicked his heart out of rhythm for a second.

The light vanished, sudden and silent, plunging Jamie into a cold darkness, leaving fuzzy white spots drifting through his vision, and when he reached the place where all the broken glass crunched under his shoes, Eric was gone.

UNDERTOW

1

Whatever Jamie expects a bar in Hawaii to be, The Alea Way is not it. Hidden off the main drag, next to a pedestrian walkway that connects two main streets, it's a narrow door covered in peeling red paint with a couple neon signs buzzing in the otherwise dark windows, and a worn brick exterior. Squeezed in between a noodle shop on one side and a narrow alley on the other.

There's nothing warm or tropical about the interior. The concrete floors are cracked and stained by years of spilled drinks.

Fly a thousand miles only to end up drinking in the same kind of shithole we have back home, Jamie thinks.

His plane had landed two hours earlier. Eric picked him up from the airport and they drove back to his apartment, had some drinks there. Jamie's thoughts were in turmoil the whole time. He hadn't yet told his brother why he'd come, why Sylvia had kicked him out.

They didn't talk about Dad. Didn't need to. Neither brother had seen him since he left. He'd walked out of their house and started another life. For all they knew, another family, too.

A couple years back, Dad had sent them letters, not long after Mom died of kidney failure, and said he wanted to reconnect. Eric burned his letter. Jamie tore his into a hundred pieces and threw it in the trash.

Guilt was a cancer, and Jamie guessed it had metastasized to the point Dad couldn't sleep anymore.

Good, Jamie thought. *I hope you never sleep again.*

He pictures their six-month old baby boy, Dylan, and how much he'd hoped something in him would change immediately when he became a father.

Eric gives the bartender a wave, a pretty woman Jamie guesses to be in her thirties. She glides from one end of the bar to the other, pouring and handing over mixed drinks and glasses of beer with practiced skill. She smiles easily and Jamie is struck by how badly he wants to talk to her.

Eric touches his elbow and guides him through a series of tables packed with men and women still dressed in work clothes—shorts stiff with fish blood, unbuttoned floral shirts worn over sweat stained wife-beaters, hands dark with grease—past a pool table leveled out with drink coasters under one leg, to a small table in the corner under a green-glass lamp made from an old buoy.

A tired-looking man close to Eric's age sits with his elbows on either side of what Jamie guesses to be Jack and Coke. He looks up and his mouth droops into a smile.

"Matty, say hey to my little brother Jamie."

Eric pulls out a chair, grabs the glass and downs half of it before Matty can stop him. Jamie shakes Matty's hand and takes the only empty seat.

"Matty's dad owns the boat I'm on," Eric says, his eyes moving around the room. His voice is light but the skin between his eyebrows is folded, intense. He gives Matty's shoulder a squeeze. "This guy works half as fast as I do, but he's good company."

Matty shrugs off the hand and makes a move to swipe back his drink, but it's a clumsy attempt and most of the liquid splashes out on the table, runs off the edge onto Matty's shorts.

The chair scrapes as he backs up, hands out. "Fucking asshole," he says, still smiling.

Eric stands, eyes scanning from table to table, face to face.

"I'll get you another," he says. Then to Jamie, "You want anything?"

"Beer," Jamie says. "Something local."

Eric nods without looking at him and makes his way to the bar. Jamie is alone with Matty, who takes too long to blink and smells like weed.

"You grow up here?" Jamie asks.

Matty's head turns slowly and his half-closed eyes meet Jamie's. He nods.

"This doesn't look like the kind of place you can get a Mai Tai inside a pineapple," Jamie says.

Matty's nose wrinkles. "That shit's for tourists."

The walls are covered with sepia-toned photographs in dirty glass frames. Old boats and grizzled men holding large fish. A massive marlin hangs above the bar, so slick and shiny Jamie can't tell if it's real or not. A pair of red panties dangle from the fish's spike. Its glossy, dead eye looks surprised.

Even from across the room, Jamie can hear Eric's laugh as he leans against the bar and chats with the pretty bartender. The smile she gives Eric looks a little more real than the one she gives the other guys. Eric slaps some money on the counter as she hands over the glasses, and Eric does a little dance to avoid bumping into other customers as he makes his way back to the table.

He sets down another Jack and Coke in front of Matty and says, "Here you go, you whiny little bitch. And for the kid," sliding Jamie a glass filled with frothy gold liquid, "a local brew."

Eric raises his glass and says, "To my little brother. It's really good to see you."

Jamie and Matty raise their own, clink them together, and drink.

"Oh," Matty says, "Evangeline poured heavy." He bats his eyelashes at Eric. "Just for you. All those other suckers have to buy two drinks to get this much booze."

Eric smiles distantly. His seat faces the door, and he keeps looking up every time it opens, like he's expecting someone.

"This your first time here?" Matty asks Jamie.

"Yeah," Jamie says. "Always wanted to visit, just never found the time."

"You don't find time," Matty says, and takes another drink. His head wobbles a little, then straightens. "It's just right there waiting for you. You know?" He burps silently and his eyes open wider. "So, what's the plan?"

Jamie looks to his brother to answer, but he's still scoping out the bar.

"Pearl Harbor, for sure," Jamie says, "and Eric mentioned something about snorkeling at Diamond Head."

Matty nods his approval. "Hitch a ride on a turtle," he mumbles.

An old feeling, something Jamie hasn't felt since junior high school, comes creeping up on him like a chill. A sense that being with his brother isn't enough, that Eric's attention will always be somewhere else.

He remembers the first time Eric took him to a party when he was a freshman and Eric was a senior. Jamie looked up to his brother, wanted to be like him. To Jamie, he was the definition of cool. He had no shortage of friends, of girls who wanted to go out with him. Everything he did was so effortless, like he had a clearer sense of who he was in the world than anyone else around him.

Jamie walked into that party with his brother, hoping to catch just a corner of the glow that surrounded him, but the moment they stepped into the house, Eric floated away with one friend or another, leaving Jamie by himself in a room filled with people he didn't know.

He felt outside the energy, the urgency of whatever was happening. A hundred tiny dramas unfolded before his eyes (a fight, girls in tears, one guy got slapped) but he didn't understand any of it. His brother was part of a world, an ecosystem, that had been in motion for three years by the time Jamie showed up at the school.

Matty is saying something about paddleboarding when the door opens and two guys walk in. They're both wearing clothes nicer than anyone else in the bar. The tall one in front wears a button-down shirt the color of the sky, beige shorts, and a pair of white shoes. His brown hair looks blow-dried. His friend is similarly dressed.

The tall one stops for a second, squints and lets his eyes adjust to the dim room. He looks over, makes eye contact with Eric, gives a small nod, and makes his way to the pool table.

"What was that waterfall you mentioned?" Jamie asks.

Eric nods slowly, as though he hears Jamie's voice but not the question. He keeps watching the two guys at the pool table as the shorter one racks up the balls and the taller one holds up a cue stick to see how straight it is.

"Waimano," Matty says. "Likeke. You should take him to Ahua Reef." His eyes float over to Jamie and he says, "Eric passed out there a few nights ago. Woke up with a mouthful of sand."

"Had too much to drink," Eric says.

Matty laughs. "You said you were sober."

"Doesn't matter. I fell asleep is all, woke up a few hours later."

"Yeah, yeah," Matty says.

Eric nods again, or maybe he hasn't stopped. Jamie notices the bartender watching him as she pours liquor into a blender and pulverizes whatever is inside. She looks sad. Worried maybe.

At the table next to them, a group of four men and one woman erupt into laughter. The woman sits on the lap of a guy with a large belly and foam in his beard, and cackles like an animal. Another man slams his hand on the table, causing all the glasses to jump.

Eric takes a small sip from his drink, sets it back down, and raps his knuckles on the table. "I'm gonna play some pool."

Matty looks at the two guys and snorts, finishes his drink, and makes his fingers spider-crawl toward Eric's glass. Eric pulls it away, stands, and heads across the room.

Jamie watches Matty's face crease as Eric stands off to the side and watches the newcomers break (shorter one takes solids) and sink a few balls.

"You know them?" Jamie asks.

Matty turns his red eyes to Jamie and nods. He spins his glass in a slow circle.

"Tall dude's A.J. Zanich. A fucking asshole. Mom's a surgeon, Dad's a real estate guy, owns like ten beach-front properties he leases to hotels. If you've ever wondered what it'd be like to have everything you wanted," Matty jerks his head, "that's what it looks like. Short dude is Kelly. Probably the only real friend A.J. has."

"This doesn't seem like their kind of place." Jamie says.

Matty's eyes, big and wet, remind Jamie of an infant who's just finished bawling. He glances at the bar, watches Evangeline move with such grace that the motions of grabbing bottles and pouring liquid, sliding glasses and taking credit cards begin to look choreographed.

"A.J. got a thing for her?" Jamie asks.

Matty sighs. "Not anymore. I've known that girl for years, and I've tried at least a thousand times to ask her out. Not in a gross way, you know? Like a real date. Dinner, a walk on the beach." He turns to Jamie, "She's an amazing person. Single mom, if you can believe it. What we're seeing right now, all those smiles, the laughing, none of it's real. She turns it on to get the tips. I don't blame her. But she's more than that, she's—"

Matty stops himself and smiles, like he's said more than he meant to.

He juts his chin toward the pool table. "The first time that asshole comes in here, he asks her out. They date for like six months, then he dumps her. She didn't come to work for days after that."

Matty's mouth tightens as he watches A.J. eye up a shot. The billiards clack together and scatter across the felt. A.J. let's out an "Oh!" as one of the balls sinks into a pocket.

"She doesn't want him here," Matty says. "Look how she's not looking at him."

Matty is right. Evangeline's body language has changed. Her movements are more rigid the smiles she gives are tighter. Her eyes flicker occasionally, to see if he's still there, if he's looking at her.

Eric stands off to the side, watching the game unfold. He lifts his glass and Jamie catches his mouth moving right before he takes a drink.

"Is Eric friends with A.J.?" Jamie asks.

Matty watches Evangeline with a pained expression. "Nah," he says. "Not friends."

He stares for a while without blinking, then shakes his head once and turns to Jamie. "You got someone?"

Jamie, surprised at the question, answers honestly. "Sort of."

Matty whistles. "And she let you come to Hawaii without her?"

"Things aren't…they aren't good right now."

"Ah, sorry about that," Matty says. "Kids?"

"One. He's still a baby."

Matty nods. "That's good. I mean, if he's young enough he won't know how to miss you yet."

He spins his glass again, mesmerized by the geometric shapes of light that shimmer in a small puddle of spilled water on the table.

"My dad and I moved from Idaho when I was seven. Mom had…problems. We've been here since. It's a good place to figure things out. Hard to be too down when the sun is shining."

Jamie takes a drink and hopes Matty is right.

Kelly, the short one, loses the game and hands the pool cue over to Eric, who takes it and twists a square of blue chalk on the end, then blows it off. A.J. racks the balls again and chalks his own cue while Eric stands at the end of the table, leans over, and takes aim.

"Your dad owns the boat, right?" Jamie asks, keeping an eye on the game.

"Yeah, twenty-seven-footer called the *Full Speed Ed*. We mostly catch tuna," Matty says, writing something in the spilled drink on the table. His finger moves through the liquid, parting it for a split second before the space fills back in and the message is lost. "Someday, we want to expand, get a second boat and double our money. Dad even mentioned making Eric captain of a third boat, if he sticks around long enough."

Eric sinks the blue-striped 10 ball and A.J. stands up straighter, his eyes a little wider, as Eric lines up his next shot.

"We'd call our second boat *Damn the Torpedoes*," Matty says.

Jamie must look confused, because Matty adds, "My dad is Ed. Damn the torpedoes, full speed ahead? *Full Speed Ed?*"

"Oh!" Jamie laughs, to be polite. "Eric says you taught him the ropes."

Matty uses the sleeve of his shirt to wipe off the table, and Jamie thinks he does it so Evangeline won't have to.

"He knew how to fish," Matty says. "But there's a huge difference between fishing and commercial fishing."

"I bet. Two weeks out at a time?"

"Sometimes longer, depending. It's a living but it ain't *living*," Matty says, like it's a phrase he heard someone else use but doesn't fully understand.

A.J. isn't smiling anymore. He stares right at Eric, watching him bring the stick back, then forward, back again, and drive it into the cue ball. It slams into the side, bounces off, and clacks into the 13 ball, sending it to the far end of the table. A.J. moves closer as the cue ball careens off into a corner pocket.

Eric straightens up and shrugs. His right hand reaches into the back pocket of his shorts, and comes out again with a small, clear baggie held between two fingers, half-filled with something white, like a magic trick. A motion that takes only a second. That same hand slips into the corner pocket and emerges holding the cue ball, but the baggie is gone.

Jamie glances over to see if Matty noticed, but he's busy gazing at Evangeline with a love-sick expression that looks almost painful.

Jamie's hands clench and unclench.

Eric moves aside as A.J. takes his place at the end of the table. Kelly sits on a tall stool against the wall, looking out at the bar. A.J.'s lips tighten as he lines up his shot. Jamie thinks he looks tenser than he should be. The game just started.

A.J. takes the shot, hitting harder than he needs to. The cue ball fires across the table and slams into the 8 ball, sending it straight into the side pocket. He tosses the stick on the felt and throws up his hands. Jamie can't hear him say it, but sees his lips form the word "shit."

He walks around the table, trailing one hand along the wooden edge. As he nears the corner pocket, his hand dips in quickly and comes out holding the baggie. He quickly shoves it into his shorts and tries to act upset at his loss (not so upset that it draws attention) but to Jamie it just comes off as bad acting.

Eric looks unfazed. He grabs the stick off the table and hangs it back in the rack on the wall while A.J. waves a hand at Kelly, like "come on, let's go," and Kelly jumps off the stool, looking nervously around the bar as they head out the door. Evangeline watches them leave, and Jamie is pretty sure she lets out a deep breath.

As Eric crosses the room, a young guy backs his chair up and almost hits Eric. His brow instantly folds into that expression Jamie knows well. The "I'm tougher than you and I will fuck you up" look that's gotten him into hundreds of fights. It's far more aggressive than the situation requires.

The young guy apologizes and moves out the way, a surprised and fearful look on his face.

Eric comes back to the table and sits. He slaps Matty's shoulder. "You're staring."

He catches Jamie watching him and shakes his head. "Don't say it. Not here."

Jamie leans back and sighs, grabs his drink and finishes what's left. He doesn't understand how his brother isn't nervous after what he just did. *He's* nervous.

Reckless.

Hasn't he always been that way? Ever since they were kids and that recklessness was climbing to the tops of trees with branches so thin they'd snap under Eric's weight. Echoing like a gunshot through the woods as his body fell five, ten feet before slamming to a stop on a more solid branch. And he'd sit there bleeding and laughing. The recklessness was stealing money from Mom's purse to buy candy and soda, or lighting a firecracker and holding it until the fuse burned almost all the way down. It was kissing the prettiest girl in school when she didn't expect it.

The recklessness became less innocent as Eric grew older and turned into the kinds of things that could get him killed. It became driving too fast, drinking too much, getting into fights, trying whatever drugs he could get his hands on.

There were drugs in the baggie, Jamie knows that much. He just doesn't know what kind of drugs. And does that even make a difference? It does to him. There is a chasm between weed and cocaine, and another between coke and heroin, and a darker chasm from that to meth.

Eric leans in the chair, one arm slung over the back, two legs tipped off the ground. One small push and he'd fall over, and if that wasn't a picture of his whole life.

"What now?" Matty asks, one elbow on the table, chin resting in the hand.

Eric hums, then says, "I was thinking we'd head down to the beach. You know the spot a mile east where the streetlights are still out? You can see millions of stars from there. So many you can almost feel them."

Matty snorts. "Feel them?"

Eric waves his hand, "I don't know, they feel closer. Like they're pressing down on us."

Stargazing sounds better to Jamie than hanging around a dive bar and watching his brother slip drugs to a rich kid while his friend makes goo-goo eyes at the bartender.

Eric finishes the rest of his drink. Says, "Ready kid?"

Jamie finishes his beer and nods.

Kid.

Always kid. For as long as Jamie can remember. It bothered him for what, two, three years in junior high? Back when he wanted to be a man as soon as possible. He grew to like it though, because it was a rare display of affection from his brother. An acknowledgement that no matter how distant, and different they might become, Jamie was always Eric's kid brother and that meant something. A kind of metallic bond that may rust over time but would always be there.

Eric rises, grabs a handful of Matty's shirt and pulls him up. Jamie stands, slides in their three chairs, and looks back at the bar. Evangeline stares right at him as she fills a pint glass from the tap. She gave a little wave and Jamie is the only one who sees it.

He waves back and smiles.

She smiles and it's beautiful.

2

The air outside is cooler than in the bar but still warm. The salty scent of the ocean drifts on a soft breeze, and the sound of it — the low rumble and static-like touch of wave to shore — is present all around. Palm trees sway gently, their fronds rustling. Some street musicians play one block down, a drummer and saxophonist putting together something like jazz infused with hip-hop. Tourists, Jamie guesses, dressed in flowing skirts, clean-collared shirts, with flowered leis around their necks, fill the streets. Wandering in and out of restaurants and bars, taking pictures, smiling, laughing.

"The hotel crowd," Eric says, quietly. "Burning through money like they won't even notice the dip in their bank accounts."

There is no bitterness in his voice. Just reality. Some people planned vacations, bought plane tickets, made hotel reservations. And some people, like Jamie and Eric, agonize over every dollar because the way they earn it is backbreaking.

They turn down the brick lined side street that leads back to the main drag, when Jamie hears someone yelling. Scared. Frantic.

"Hey, come on man, wake up."

He touches Eric's arm and he stops, about to say something when he hears it too.

"Kelly! Fuck! Wake up."

Matty walks a few steps, spins in place, mouth falling open, eyes opening wider.

"Shit. Shit. Kelly! Fuck man, come on."

The voice comes from the alleyway next to the bar. A space narrow enough that Jamie could touch both walls if he spreads his arms out.

"Is that…?" he starts to say when Eric nods and hold a finger to his lips.

A.J.

Eric silently points to one side of the alley and Jamie jogs over to the other wall, sneaking a quick glance down the dark stretch of unlit alley. He takes his place and Eric stands on the other side, head cocked. Listening.

The voice gets quieter, then stops, replaced by fast exhales in quick succession, the kind of breathing that makes Jamie think of Sylvie when she was in labor with their son. She squeezed his hand so hard it was sore for days.

Eric holds up one hand, waits, then motions for them to go. The brothers enter the alley, their shadows stretching across a rectangle of light that cuts in from the street and find A.J. Zanich kneeling over a body lying on the ground, surrounded by black trash bags and Styrofoam food containers. A.J. has both hands pressed to Kelly's chest and he's breathing heavy, whispering, "God damn it, shit, fuck," between each push.

Jamie doesn't know CPR, but he saw it performed once at the docks when a co-worker went down with a heart attack. One of the crane operators, a six-foot-eight giant named Kevin who wore shorts even in the winter, started chest compressions. Jamie remembers the wet crack of bone snapping inside the man's chest as Kevin pushed, sweat dripping off his red face. The rest of the crew gathered around, unsure what to do. The supervisor paced back and forth, phone to his ear, begging for the ambulance to hurry.

Kevin later told Jamie that you often break ribs during compressions. You have to pump the heart manually, squeezing it between the sternum and spine so that oxygenated blood keeps flowing through the arteries.

Jamie has never forgotten that sound, or the way Kevin's massive hands seemed to disappear inside the unconscious man's chest, and he can tell A.J. has no clue what he's doing, and he's definitely not pushing down hard enough to do anything for Kelly's heart.

A.J. jerks away from Kelly's body when the two men enter the alley. He scrambles backward into the trash bags, mouth fluttering like a fish just pulled out of the ocean and gulping for air.

"I'm just trying to help," he says, his face a pale mask of fear. Then he recognizes Eric and the fear melts into anger. He struggles to his feet and rushes at

Eric, plants both hands against his chest and shoves hard.

"What the fuck did you give me?"

Eric stumbles back, regains his balance and moves closer to A.J. The two men are roughly the same height, but Eric's shoulders are much broader, the muscles flexing under his shirt sleeves bigger.

He holds up a finger. "Don't fucking touch me again."

A.J. points down at Kelly, who looks like he's asleep with his eyes half open.

"You did this," he says, voice shaking.

Jamie kneels next to Kelly and holds two fingers against his throat. The skin is cold and clammy. He's not sure if he's feeling in the right place, but he's hoping for a *thump thump* against his fingertips. Something to tell him the heart is still pumping.

He feels nothing.

He lowers his head next to Kelly's face, waiting for some air coming from the mouth, the nose.

He looks up at Eric and shakes his head.

A.J. fumbles in his pocket and pulls out a cellphone.

"You fucking killed him." He sounds on the verge of tears.

He stabs at the screen, but his hands shake too much and the phone falls to ground. A spiderweb cracks over the glass.

"Fuck!"

Matty stands at the alley entrance, frantically rubbing his face with both hands. He keeps looking out to the street, moving from side to side to block the view of anyone walking by.

He laughs nervously and says, "Too much to drink," to a couple as they pass by. They glance into the narrow space quickly and keep walking.

Jamie looks at his brother and sees the cords in his neck popping under the skin. Sees his hands clenched into fists, making the veins in his arms bulge. A.J. doesn't seem aware of how tense and coiled Eric is, because he takes a few steps forward, jabbing his finger close to Eric's chest.

"This is on you," he yells. "It's all on you!"

"I told you," Eric says, his voice a low growl, "I didn't know what was in there."

"You said coke," A.J. wails, pacing from side to side like he's dancing.

"The guy said it was coke. I told you I wasn't sure. You said you wanted it anyway."

"Fentanyl," Matty mutters, looking down at the ground.

Eric and A.J. don't acknowledge, but Jamie knows he's probably right. An overdose this quick, this peaceful, has to be fentanyl. Maybe laced with coke, but more of the other drug.

A.J. turns and looks down at Kelly's lifeless body, his eyes open enough to see the dilated pupils rolled back, like he's thinking of the answer to a hard question. A.J. buries his face in his hands and lets out a muffled scream.

Jamie can't tell if he's more upset about his friend's death, or the consequences of that death.

"What do we do?" A.J. asks, looking at Jamie for the first time. "We can't just leave him here."

Jamie realizes his fingers are still on Kelly's throat, against his cold skin, and he quickly pulls his hand away.

"Jamie," Eric says, "let's go."

A.J. bends down and picks up his phone. The screen lights up at his touch.

"No, no, no. This is your fault and you're fucking paying. You're not leaving me here to take the blame."

"A.J.," Eric says, holding out a hand. "Don't call. Give me the phone."

A.J. snorts and pushes a button that opens a pad of numbers. "This isn't on me. If the cops search my place, they're not gonna find shit. What about you, Eric? Will they find anything at your place?"

He taps the screen a few more times and holds the phone to his ear. Jamie blinks once and in that time, Eric has rushed forward. He slaps the phone out of AJ.'s hand and it smashes into the wall. When it hits the ground, Eric stomps on it with his heel, shattering the screen.

A.J. screams, "Fuck you," and rams his shoulder into Eric's stomach, knocking him backward.

He tries to catch his balance and falls over into a pile of garbage bags. Glass bottles pop underneath him.

Jamie wants to scream at A.J. to stop and run away, because if Eric gets up he'll start swinging and he won't stop until he's covered in blood, but everything happens too fast.

He starts to move and it feels like slow motion. Too slow. Like when he and Eric were kids and they'd lie on the floor, each of them holding onto one of Dad's ankles, and he'd walk across the house, dragging them along slowly. Back when they used to think he was so strong.

A.J. crouches and moves toward Eric. Matty stands in the alley entrance, mouth falling open, and Jamie watches Eric crawl backward through all the trash, his right hand blindly sweeping for something.

A.J. grabs Eric's shirt with one hand, cocks back the other, and punches Eric in the face with a sickening crack. Eric's head snaps to the side. The skin above his eye splits open and pours blood. Jamie is shocked that Eric let himself get hit. His right hand keeps digging around.

A camera flash goes off from the street and someone laughs. It sounds slow and deep, like the recording of a laugh playing at half-speed.

Jamie approaches A.J. from behind, is about to wrap an arm around his neck in a chokehold, when Eric's right hand comes shooting up holding something that sparkles in the neon light of a bar sign. He slices at A.J.'s neck with it and there's a sound like ripping fabric, then a gulp. A hard swallow. A.J. takes one step back, turns to Jamie, and his eyes are open so wide Jamie can see the full roundness of them.

There's a single dark line across A.J.'s neck that splits open when he finally inhales. Skin and muscle separate to reveal the red hole of his throat. Warm blood sprays out of the wound, splattering on Jamie's face, before A.J. clasps both hands to his throat and staggers against the brick wall, blood pouring between his fingers.

Surprised.

That's what Jamie thinks as he watches the man slide down the wall until his ass is on the ground, his feet jerking, kicking greasy takeout boxes and soda cups.

He's dying and he looks surprised.

Eric comes and stands over A.J., a broken beer bottle gripped in his right hand. He's breathing heavy like an animal and Jamie knew, somewhere in his head, he *knew* this wouldn't end well.

Keeping one hand on his throat, A.J. reaches out weakly with the other, a gurgling sound now coming from the hole as blood bubbles out. The movement of his legs grows weaker until it stops altogether. His outstretched arm falls, and the hand he held to his throat drops to his side. His eyes remain open, staring at the far wall.

As Jamie looks at his brother, at his clenched teeth and creased forehead, for two or three heavy heartbeats he's almost afraid Eric is going to turn and slash at him.

The bottle clatters to the brick and Eric takes a deep breath. He holds his hand up to the light, and it's dark and wet from a wide gash across the palm. The hand shakes like Parkinson's as he looks to the entrance of the alley, to the street beyond.

Matty says, "Oh shit, oh shit," over and over.

Jamie can't find words. He stands beside his brother, two dead bodies on the ground. He smells sweat and the strong metallic odor of blood.

Eric whispers, "Fuck," and rubs his face with his non-bleeding hand. He looks over and says, "Matty, come here."

Matty shuffles over, blinking furiously, chin quivering. He tries not to look at the gaping hole in A.J.'s throat, but he can't help it, and he gags when he sees the open wound like a second, toothless mouth.

"Give me your phone," Eric says, and Matty fumbles in his pocket until he finds it and hands it over, shaking so hard he almost drops it.

Eric holds up his bad hand, blood running down his arm and dripping off the elbow.

"Sit down next to him," he says.

Matty moans. "Shit man. Shit."

"You don't have to look at him, just sit there and be quiet."

Matty does as he's told. He leans his back to the wall and slides down, just like A.J. had, whimpering the whole time. He hangs both arms on his knees and buries his head. Jamie hears him gagging some more.

When Eric touches the phone, the light from the screen makes his face look ghostly pale, with splashes of black it takes Jamie a second to recognize as blood.

He knows better than to say anything. Besides, there's nothing to say.

This is bad.

Eric knows that.

You fucked up.

He knows that too.

The gears in his brother's head must be moving like the wheels on a train. Just grinding away at full speed.

Eric opens the contacts, scrolls, then hits a button and holds the phone to his ear.

A group of five or six tourists, young and drunk, wander by the entrance of the alley. A guy, smiling big with his arm around a girl, stops and squints into the alley.

"Hey," he yells. "Everything okay?"

Eric looks at Jamie, eyes wide, and nods toward the guy with a look of "take care of this," then turns away.

"We're good," Jamie yells back, trying his best to match the young man's smile. "Couple friends had too much to drink." He makes a barf face and laughs. It sounds so fake, but the guy doesn't seem to notice.

He laughs and says, "Right on!" and staggers off to rejoin his friends.

Matty keeps whimpering, "Oh shit, oh god, oh shit," like it's a mantra and Eric says into the phone, "Ed? It's Jamie. We've got a big problem."

3

Eric walks further into the alley, speaking in a low voice. He shakes his head a few times, nods, shakes again, and finally comes back.

He holds the phone out and says, "Matt."

Matt, not Matty, Jamie thinks.

Matty lifts his head, lets out a moan, and takes the phone.

"Yeah, I'm okay," he says. His voice sounds like a child's. Small and frightened. "Dad? This is really fucked up. I don't want to be here." A pause as he listens. "Yeah…yeah…okay…I will."

He hangs up, puts the phone back in his pocket, and lowers his head again.

A group of voices drifts from the street and Eric says to Jamie, "Face me, act like we're talking."

The voices get louder as people come into view. Jamie turns to his brother and has a sudden burst of fear that someone will see the blood all over his face. Eric must have had the same thought because he hunches over and starts dry heaving. Jamie pats his back, gives the group a wave as they pass by, and stops when they're gone.

"Your face," he says to Eric, when he straightens up.

Eric's mouth stretches open and cracks the hardening blood. He grabs his shirt and wipes his face with it, but the shirt is soaked in blood and just smears on his skin.

"Ed is Matty's dad," Eric says, untying the arms of the zip hoodie from around his waist. "He's coming to get us." He tosses the sweatshirt to Jamie. "Can you get the sleeves off?"

Jamie takes it, bunches one sleeve into a ball, and pulls until the seams tear apart. He gives the sleeve to Eric who wraps it around his wounded hand, hissing as he does. He then takes the hoodie and puts it on, zips it all the way so his bloodstained shirt is no longer visible.

When his eyes meet Jamie's, the intense stare is gone, replaced by something Jamie only ever sees when Eric has done something bad—not mistake-bad, but this-will-have -real-consequences-bad.

Regret.

Sadness.

"I didn't mean to do…that," Eric says. "I know I can get out of hand. Get violent. But, fuck, man, I never meant to kill him. I just wanted to hurt him, you know?"

Jamie blinks slowly and when his eyes close he sees his brother, teeth bared like a dog's, arm swinging, broken glass flashing as it cuts through A.J.'s throat. The intention and the action are separated in Eric's mind as he struggles to justify what he's done, but

Jamie knows Eric did exactly what he meant to do. His body realized it only seconds before his brain did.

Deep down, Jamie always knew his brother was capable of murder. Knew from the time they were kids. He just never believed he'd be there to witness it. He thought he'd find out in a phone call from a lawyer, or on the news.

No matter what Jamie felt, he knew it wasn't the time to start thinking about when and how Eric changed, about the million ways in which the brother he had in high school was not the same brother he had before then.

"What about the...the bodies?" Jamie asks.

Eric crosses his arms to hide his wrapped hand. He's always been strong, but the missing sleeves on the sweatshirt show lean, powerful arms forged from months of hard work at sea.

"We take A.J. and leave Kelly," Eric says. He catches Jamie's eyes and looks away quickly. "Kelly isn't our fault."

Our.

Already, the event doesn't belong to him. It transformed from red-hot melted glass to something solid and transparent in a matter of minutes. It belongs to all of them. And maybe he's right about that.

Another memory flash and Jamie thinks of being kids, how Eric could never take full responsibility for what he broke, what he stole, what he burned. The blame had to be shared, and what was a little brother for if not helping shoulder a burden?

Jamie's mind races. Too much has happened, *is* happening, for his thoughts to make sense. He barely registers the fact that they're taking AJ. Taking him where? The hospital? There's no point. And then there's the reason any of this happened at all. The baggie in the pool table.

"Did you know?" Jamie asks.

Eric tilts his head. "Know what?"

"Did you know what was in the baggie?"

The crease between the eyes comes back and it's too close to how Eric looked at A.J. for Jamie to feel comfortable. His eyes narrow and the corners of his lips curl into something almost like a snarl. He's about to answer when a shadow falls over them. They both turn to see a silhouette standing in the alleyway entrance.

A deep voice says, "Everybody okay?"

Matty lifts his head. "Dad?"

The silhouette comes closer, giving Jamie a view of a broad-chested man with a thick beard, intense eyes, and the same wide nose as his son. He wears a flannel shirt and an old Phillies baseball hat with a faded logo.

Eric nods, "We're okay, Ed."

The man glares at Jamie, from the top of his head to his shoes, then looks back to Eric.

"Jamie," he says. "My brother."

Ed nods at Eric's cradled hand wrapped in the blood-soaked fabric. "Let me see."

Eric undoes the cloth and Ed takes the hand, angles it into the light. His eyes twitch. "Keep pressure on it for now. I can stitch it up once we're on the boat."

He brushes past Jamie and marches over to Kelly's body. He kneels and leans in but doesn't touch it. He takes off his hat, wipes sweat from his brow with a sleeve, and turns to Matty. His eyes move from his son to the body sitting beside him, the entire shirt completely soaked red.

"You alright?" Ed asks.

Matty nods.

He points at A.J. and says, "You have anything to do with this?"

Eric steps forward. "He didn't do anything…"

Ed holds up a finger to silence Eric. "I'm talking to my son."

Matty shakes his head, again and again. "No, sir, I didn't."

"Is there anything here," Ed's hands sweep the alleyway, "that comes back to you?"

Matty bites his lip, fighting tears. "No, sir."

Ed groans as he stands and takes a small flashlight from his flannel pocket. He turns it on and moves the beam around the bodies, the wet brick and trash bags around them. The light picks up a small, clear baggie half full of white powder lying a few inches away from Kelly.

Ed shines the light at Jamie and he closes his eyes against the brightness of it.

"Is there anything," Ed says, "that comes back to you?"

The light moves off Jamie and onto Eric.

"The drugs were mine," Eric says, blocking the light with his good hand. "A guy gave it to me in that bag, and that's how I gave it to A.J. There isn't any at the apartment. That was all I had."

Ed clicks off the light. "And what did A.J. give you?"

Eric reaches into his back pocket and holds up two one-hundred-dollar bills folded in half. Jamie hadn't even seen that part of the transaction in the bar.

"Where did you get it?"

"I let a guy stay at the apartment for a few days last time we were out," Eric says. "He didn't have enough cash to cover it, so he gave me that," nodding to the baggie. "I thought it was coke."

"Who's the guy?" Ed asks.

"Nixon."

"Nixon Kekoa?"

Eric nods.

"That fuckin' asshole," Ed says. "That's good, though. Everyone knows he deals."

The flashlight turns back on and shines on the ground. Ed lifts one shoe from a puddle of blood. "What a fuckin' mess." He sighs. "Okay, let's get A.J. out of here."

4

Once, when Jamie and Eric's parents were still together, they took a family trip to the beach. The Oregon Coast, though beautiful, is known for its cold water and rocky shoreline. Thankfully, the day was sunny rather than the usual gray clouds and overcast sky, and the two adults set out a blanket while the boys played in the water. Jamie would have been six at the time.

Right before he ran into the ocean, Jamie's mother told him to be careful because of the undertow. He said he would, but he had no idea what she was talking about.

After an hour of trying to jump over the frothy rush of incoming waves, Jamie lost his balance and fell in the cold water. The shock of being fully submerged stole his breath, and he swallowed a mouthful of salty water.

While he scrambled for the surface, he felt something like a strong hand grip his leg and yank him under even further. He kicked his legs, frantically trying to find the sandy bottom. and when his feet touched down, he launched himself up, his head breaking through to the air.

His arms flailed as he yelled for help. He turned in a circle and the shore seemed so much further away than it had been when he went under. Eric was just a small figure wading back to the sand.

Jamie yelled again, and again, but that giant hand grabbed his legs and jerked his body beneath the surface. Waves crashed over him, sending his body spinning through darkness.

He swam as hard as he could, but he didn't know if he was going up or down.

Water stung his eyes and his lungs burned for oxygen.

Was he getting closer or further from shore?

When he thought he couldn't hold his breath anymore, he stopped fighting and let himself sink. He opened his eyes as his body slowly drifted down. Sunlight broke through the water above him, growing dimmer and dimmer the deeper it went.

At the moment his chest felt like it was going to explode, Jamie's feet touched sand and he launched himself up again. But he wasn't strong enough. The sun dappled water was just out of reach. Then, a strong hand gripped him again and, rather than pulling him down, lifted him up.

His head broke the surface, and the light was so bright all he saw were two dark shapes carrying him back to shore. It wasn't until he fell onto the sand, exhausted and breathless, that he recognized Dad and Eric beside him.

Jamie had nightmares for weeks after that. In his dreams he'd feel those cold hands wrap around his ankles and pull him somewhere he did not want to go.

Undertow.

Caught in something that's pulling him under, deeper and deeper into the dark.

He feels like that now as Ed instructs him and Eric to lift up A.J. Zanich's lifeless body, one of them under each arm to support it. Ed then unbuttons and takes off his flannel shirt, runs A.J.'s limp arms through the holes and buttons it back up to cover as much of the blood as he can. He takes off his Phillies hat and puts it on A.J.'s head, pulling the brim down low to hide his face.

Ed tells Matty where he parked the truck—two blocks away on a side street—and instructs him to drop the tailgate and cover the bed with the tarp in back.

Once Matty leaves the alley, Ed turns to the brothers, standing with the dead man hanging between them like he's crucified, and says, "Walk out of here like he's so drunk he can't walk. Don't look at anyone and don't stop for anything. Keep his feet on the ground, smile if you can. Just keep moving until you get to the truck. Each of you, one arm around his shoulders, one around his back."

Ed goes to the edge of the alley, peers around the corner, and holds up a hand. As soon as a couple men come into view, Ed says loudly enough for them to hear, "Alright, let's get the drunk bastard home. Fuckin' asshole, passing out on the street. Shit."

The men look over and Ed lifts his hands and shrugs, like *what are you gonna do?* Jamie and Eric wait until the men are out of view, then follow Ed into the street.

The body is heavier than Jamie expects. He's helped carry more than his fair share of drunk friends to a car, upstairs to an apartment, but all of them had some level of consciousness. A.J. is dead weight, and Jamie notices this most in the shoulders, the way they bend upward more than they should, like the joint is going to come tearing right out of the socket.

A car passes and they are momentarily bathed in the glow of headlights. Jamie squints against the brightness.

They take a few steps and Jamie has to readjust. A.J.'s left arm is slung over his shoulder, and he grips the cold wrist with one hand to hold the arm in place. He slides his other arm down to A.J.'s waist and grabs a handful of shorts to keep him from slipping down.

Eric is struggling, too. Breathing heavy and cursing quietly. The tips of A.J.'s shoes scratch along the brick.

Ed walks ahead of them, slowly, trying to look casual.

Two girls, shuffling in a crooked line onto the side street, laugh so loud their voices bounce off the walls. Ed pauses as they near him. He gives a quick nod, and when they pass he waves for Jamie and Eric to keep moving.

As the girls get closer, Jamie notices their glossy eyes, their crooked smiles. One girl, who smells of too much perfume, carrying a single shoe with a broken heel by the strap (the other still on her foot) walks with a pronounced limp. When she sees the three men, she sticks out her bottom lip and says, "Poor baby. Get him home to mommy."

Then she laughs. Her friend joins in, and they hold hands as they wander off to the busier part of the city.

The muscles in Jamie's arms start to cramp. He adjusts his grip on A.J.'s shorts and hears Eric make a gagging cough as the rhythm of their slow walk gets knocked off. Jamie is about to ask if he's okay when he notices the smell coming from A.J.'s body. Shit and piss and the metallic tang of blood.

Jamie's stomach gurgles and twists. He breathes through his mouth, but he still feels the acid boiling in his guts. The body sags on Eric's side, almost pulling Jamie off balance. He can't see his brother's face, but hears the hard swallow of air as Eric's gagging gets louder.

A siren wails in the distance and Jamie has a sick feeling that a cop car is going to be screeching around the corner, and men in uniform will jump out, guns drawn. But the lonely howl fades and the two men keep moving.

A.J.'s body shifts again and suddenly Jamie is supporting all the weight by one arm as Eric doubles over. He retches and vomit splashes on the ground.

Jamie hears and feels a loud pop from A.J.'s shoulder and his sweaty hands can't hold him any longer. The arm slips out of his grip and the body drops facedown to the pavement. The head smacks the concrete with a sound like a cantaloupe falling off a kitchen counter. He hears a sickening crack, too.

Ed stops and turns around, his face contorts. He looks mad enough to come and hoist A.J. up in a fireman's carry himself. He looks past Eric, both arms wrapped around his stomach as he continues throwing up, to a group of college-aged partiers coming down the street.

Ed jogs toward Jamie, saying, "Shit, you guys alright?"

The group sees Eric, and the puddle of vomit under his shoes, and keep as far away as they can. Only one guy looks at Jamie and his eyes are clearer than the others.

Probably the designated driver.

But he doesn't say anything. He just keeps watching and walking, and Jamie thinks he'd probably be able to ID all of them if the police got involved.

"Those are them, officer. The three men with the dead body."

Ed says louder than he needs to, "We've gotta get you boys to the hospital. Come on, pick him up."

He kneels next to A.J.'s motionless body, like he's checking on him, and as soon as the group rounds the corner out of view, Ed grabs Eric's arm and pulls him upright. Eric spits off to the side, his face pale.

"Pick him up," Ed says, then glares at Jamie, as if he's the one responsible for letting the body fall.

Eric blinks and shakes his head a few times, then reaches down for A.J.'s arm. Jamie does the same and they slip the arms back over their shoulders. Ed helps by pushing on A.J.'s chest until he's suspended between the brothers again.

Jamie glances over at the dead man's face and immediately wishes he hadn't. The nose is flattened against the cheek, and the orbital socket has been shattered, giving the face an unnerving putty-like appearance, like the man's skin has melted, and the eyeball floats inside this mass of flesh, the pupil off-center.

A bird flies overhead and lets out a call that sounds like a woman's scream. A chill crawls over Jamie's scalp.

Ed scowls, comes behind A.J., grabs the waistband of his shorts, and lifts his dangling feet off the pavement. "Let's go," Ed growls, and the three men start walking as fast as they can, Ed shooting looks behind him to see if anyone is watching.

Matty is waiting at the truck (an older gray four-door with patches of rust where the paint has cracked), tailgate down and tarp spread out just like Ed wanted. Jamie shifts to grab under both arms as Eric grabs hold of the legs, and with Ed pushing up on A.J.'s back they lift the body. Jamie's instinct is to set him down gently, and it's only when Ed and Eric let go that Jamie realizes it doesn't matter. He moves his hands and lets the body crash lifelessly onto the truck bed, the back of the skull bouncing off the hard surface with a dull *thunk*.

Ed grabs the edge of the tarp and pulls it up over A.J.'s cloudy eyes, his smashed nose, then rolls him inside the blue material that crinkles like dried leaves.

Ed slams the tailgate and heads to the driver's side. Matty and Jamie get in the back seat while Eric goes to the passenger side. The engine rumbles to life and Ed eases out onto the road, driving so much slower than Jamie thinks he should. They're leaving a crime scene.

He doesn't want to think of the word *murder*.

But that's what it is.

They drive in silence. Except for their breathing. Four men inhaling and exhaling with a combination of exertion and fear.

They roll to a stop under a streetlight and Eric's face is lit from the side. Jamie stares at the shape of his profile and is reminded of those nights when Sleep Eric climbed down from the top bunk and stood in the moonlight.

We share blood.

Under any other circumstances, Jamie would be terrified of the man sitting in that seat. A man who slashed the throat of another human less than thirty minutes ago, now staring out the window with lips pressed together, one hand rubbing absently at his buzzed hair.

That feeling again, of being pulled under.

He's my brother.

He's a murderer.

Both things are true, but Jamie can only hold on to one thought at a time, and his mind dances back and forth between them.

He wants to protect Eric, and he wants to be as far away from him as he can get.

Matty is curled up against the window like a child, covering his face with a hand and trying not to cry. Ed breathes heavy, in and out through his nose, like a hibernating bear. He veers onto side streets, driving away from the active main drag, away from the tourists and nightlife.

Jamie isn't supposed to leave for another five days, but he wonders if he can go to the airport, get his ticket changed and catch an earlier flight.

He sees beyond this night, to the next day and the day after, and he has no idea how he'll be able to face Eric. How he could look at his brother and not see a killer? And beyond that, weeks, months, years from now, how will Jamie face him? Do they carry this secret all the way to the end?

Jamie blinks hard and feels the burn of tears in his eyes.

Whatever happens next, he and Eric will never be the same. And he feels that loss already. The events of the night have separated the ground between them. Where Jamie wants to be, and where Eric is, are so far apart that nothing could possibly bridge that chasm.

5

The truck moves slowly down a steep road with a clear view of the ocean glittering like a dark diamond under the pale light of a half-moon. The horizon is a black line dividing the water from the deep blue sky.

The clouds look like shredded cotton glowing at the edges, and makes Jamie think of their dog (that died not long after Dad left) who tore apart one of Eric's stuffed animals, and left the stuffing scattered all over his room.

Matty sniffs and lets out a small moan. Ed jerks around in his seat and glares at his son until the sound stops. Eric stares out the windshield with a blank expression. Clouds drift apart to reveal stars twisting over black sky.

Soon, the harbor comes into view - narrow docks jutting out into the water like the ribs of a skeleton, with boats moored on either side. It's mostly dark, but a few of the boats have yellow lights glowing from small windows.

The truck crawls down more side streets. Ed doesn't have the AC going and the air inside the cab becomes stifling. They turn a corner and Jamie feels a thump from the truck bed, and he tries not to picture

A.J.'s lifeless body rolling around back there. The thought makes his stomach twist like he's got the shits.

Ed pulls onto a small road that runs alongside a pier. He makes a right at the far end and parks. Behind them lies the harbor, and in front of them only vast, open ocean. Ed turns the key and they all sit in silence, except for the sound of the engine ticking.

Ed peers out at the dark water, the moon reflecting off its surface like a warped spotlight.

He rubs a hand along his chin, and the scratching sound makes Jamie think of insect legs.

Still looking straight ahead, Ed says, "When you end up with two dead boys in an alley, someone started it." He turns to Eric. "So, who started it?"

Eric faces Ed, and Jamie sees them both in profile, and through the windshield the ocean is so close it almost feels like they're already on a boat. Jamie's stomach lifts a little in rhythm with the water.

"He came at me," Eric says, his voice calm. "He pushed me down, punched me once, and was getting ready to hit me again."

Ed twists in his seat, looks right at Jamie. "That true?"

Jamie nods without saying anything. Swallows, then adds, "Yes, sir."

Ed turns to Matty. "True?"

Matty nods his head and keeps nodding until Ed yells, "Hey! I'm not fuckin' around, here. I want a 'yes' or 'no' when I ask you a question. So, which is it?"

Matty moans and sniffs some more, and for a second, Jamie is afraid Full Speed Ed is going to come crawling over the seat to shake the answer out of his son.

"Yes…sir," Matty finally manages.

Ed sighs and turns back around. The seat creaks with his weight.

Jamie's heartbeat feels so big and heavy he wonders if everyone else can hear it, thumping away like a wheelbarrow with a flat tire.

"Before we go any further, I need to make one thing clear," Ed says. "What we're doing here is fixing a problem. Sometimes, you gotta do something that don't feel right because everything else is wrong."

He breathes out, deep. "Once we're done with this, we don't say a goddamn word about it, ever. Are we clear on that?"

Ed's eyes go big as he looks at Eric first. Eric meets his eyes and nods, then looks back out the window. Ed turns to Jamie, then Matty. They both nod and Ed says, "Okay. Matt, go over to the office and make sure the harbor master isn't awake. Then meet us at the boat."

Matty makes a sound like a small, wounded animal, and Ed lowers his voice. "Matthew, did you hear what I said?"

"Yes, sir."

He opens the door and stumbles out, making his way toward the long rectangular building Jamie assumes is the office.

Ed waits a moment, his sweaty hands twisting the steering wheel.

"Okay," he says. "Let's go."

The three men exit the truck and move to the back. Ed takes a look around first, then lowers the tailgate, and he and Eric grab the tarp and pull it toward them. A hand falls out and dangles off the edge of the tailgate like the pale belly of a fish. The sight of it makes Jamie feel like he's going to vomit.

Ed puts a hand on Eric's shoulder. "Carry him, same as before. We don't care if we're seen. Some of these guys," nodding to the other boats, "have a few beers top deck and watch the weather. Just a drunk friend, yeah? Getting him on the boat."

A few yellow lights ripple on the surface of the harbor. A radio plays classic rock and someone laughs. Jamie hears water lap against the boats as they gently rock with the current, the rubber buoys squeaking along the dock. A seagull squawks from atop a mast.

"I'll meet you there," Ed says, and he takes off at a brisk walk toward the boats.

Jamie is left alone with Eric, and he's not prepared for the fear he feels being this close to his brother. Shoulder to shoulder. Close enough to smell his sweat, an odor that makes him think of the childhood bedroom they shared for so many years. Piles of dirty laundry, posters pulled out of music magazines and tacked to the walls (but only after Dad left—he had no problem putting his fist through a wall, but the little hole from a thumbtack would make him crazy).

If he was anyone else, I wouldn't be here.

"Where would you be?" he almost says out loud.

Probably handcuffed in a police station, spilling the whole story. Knowing that whatever direction his life was going to take would be completely different. A deviation from the line that was his future. But he'd accept that, willingly, to avoid carrying the guilt he knew in his guts was waiting for them by the time this was over.

He's already starting to feel the sharp claws of it scratching up his spine. The fear is stronger, though. A powerline wrapped in razor wire twisting around his lungs.

The ocean tide hisses along the shoreline, a woman hushing a baby to sleep, and Jamie wants to close his eyes, drift away to somewhere this isn't happening.

Accident or not, Eric murdered A.J. and Jamie couldn't think of it as self-defense. A.J. was going to punch him, sure. But Eric opened up the guy's throat. The two things were not equal.

How can you do those things without it eating away at you? Ten, twenty, thirty years from now, Jamie will still remember every detail about this night. And he knows it. He'll remember every word, every sight, sound, and smell. It's part of him now.

Dumping a body? Protecting a murderer?

He grinds the sole of his shoe on the pavement, bends his foot a little, and imagines taking off through the dark. Running past all the boats, up the road, and not stopping until he finds someone, anyone, who can drive him straight to the cops.

Eric's voice startles him. "Ready?"

Jamie croaks out a "Yeah," and Eric tugs the tarp until the body inside begins to roll. Jamie watches his brother as he bunches up the tarp and tosses it, then grabs A.J.'s arm and pulls him upright, rough, like he's nothing more than a large tuna.

The body sits on the edge of the tailgate, head drooping. Jamie gets on the other side and lifts A.J.'s arm (which feels surprisingly heavy) and drapes it over his shoulder. The brothers stand with the body hung between them again and do their strange dance toward the dock.

Jamie catches sight of Matty jogging in their direction. He goes past, wheezing for breath as he heads down to the dock. He doesn't say anything, so Jamie assumes the harbor master is asleep.

Eric knows exactly where he's going, so Jamie lets him lead. They turn onto the first dock and follow Matty to the second boat from the end. Thankfully, none of the other ships moored here have their lights on, and there aren't any silhouettes sitting on the decks.

Sweat traces down Jamie's back. His muscles burn and he realizes he's still treating this body like a person, like someone who can feel pain. He digs his fingertips hard into the cold flesh to keep the arm from slipping out of his grip, and his stomach lunges up into his throat.

A single dim light glows from the boat up ahead, enough for Jamie to see the words *Full Speed Ed* painted on the bow.

The edge of the deck is higher than the pier, and there's a small gap where the water is visible between them. There's no easy way to get the body on board. Not without a large piece of wood to use as a ramp.

Ed and Matty come and lean over the deck, and Ed whispers, "Just let him go. We'll pull him up."

Jamie and Eric get as close as they can, and after Eric says, "One, two, three," the brothers let go of A.J.'s body. It falls straight forward and the chest slams into the edge of the deck, causing the head to snap so far back Jamie swears the hair touches the spine. Ed and Matty each grab an arm and pull the body, dragging it up and over until it falls onto the deck.

Eric unties the mooring ropes, tosses them into the boat, then jumps on board. Jamie follows, his legs already weak and rubbery, and once he's on the boat, the feeling gets even worse.

Ed disappears into the wheelhouse, and a few seconds later Jamie feels the engine rumble to life under his feet.

The boat backs away from the dock and trudges quietly past a dozen other boats, floating empty and silent, as Ed guides them out into the dark vastness of the ocean.

6

Jamie has never been on a boat in the ocean, and isn't prepared for the power of it, the feeling that most of the earth's surface is covered in miles of water. Entire mountain ranges rise up under the surface, crushed beneath the immeasurable weight of what they now sail on.

He hears the screech of metal hinges and turns to see Eric lifting a hatch at the center of the deck. A blast of cold air comes rushing out.

"Help me get him in," Eric says, bending down and grabbing one of A.J.'s arms. Jamie grabs the other arm and they drag the body to the edge of a dark hole. A light flickers on, off, and on again, and illuminates a large freezer. Ice glistens from the bottom, tinted red with fish blood. Jamie shivers as the cold moves over his skin.

Eric pushes the body until the arms and head hang over the lip of the freezer. Then he grips A.J.'s shorts and shoves him all the way through. The corpse falls six feet and crashes into a bed of ice, lying there with the head spun almost all the way around, the misshapen eye staring up through the hatch to the stars above. One arm is twisted so the hand points the wrong direction.

Just when Jamie thinks he's about to throw up, Eric slams the hatch shut and sits on it. His chest heaves as he catches his breath. He looks up and catches Jamie's eye and they stare at each other. Ever since they were kids, Eric only had to look at him and he knew exactly what his brother was thinking. Like telepathy. There is one person in the world Jamie can't hide from, and that's Eric. He doesn't even have to say anything, he just stares, first at Jamie's eyes, then at his forehead, like he can peer right through the skull and see his thoughts playing like a movie.

Eric's elbows rest on his knees. His breath comes quick and shallow. He lifts one hand and taps the side of his head with a finger.

He says, "Don't look at me like that."

Jamie doesn't need to ask, "Like what?" He feels his face changing shape to reflect all the turmoil in him. Muscles twitching, skin folding along his brow like a line of waves coming into shore. Each heartbeat, each hard swallow, makes the flesh knot between his eyes. Every second that passes adds a little more weight to whatever this night will eventually become. Whatever he'll have to carry. He's never been as cold as Eric.

But that's not entirely true. Eric wasn't always like this. Not until he started sleepwalking.

"We'll deal with all this later," Eric says, digging the finger into his temple. "Right now, we have to outrun what we're feeling and take care of this."

And there's that *we* again.

And again, he's not wrong.

Jamie wants it all to be on Eric but it's not. Maybe he set it in motion, or maybe he didn't, either way this thing has a momentum that carries all of them, and Jamie knows that whatever happens after this is "taken care of" will be the end of something.

How can I ever look at him again? How can I look at myself?

And there it is, the bloody beating heart at the center of everything. For years, Jamie wanted to be like Eric. Until the year he started sleepwalking. The year he *changed*. At some point, once Jamie realized his brother was selfish and angry, he decided he wanted to be *better* than Eric.

But here they are. On the boat together, and it isn't just Eric's fingerprints bruised on A.J.'s arms. It isn't just Eric's clothes that are stained with A.J.'s blood.

A trigger man and a getaway driver.

That's the blade at the bottom of the blender that's pulverizing all his thoughts. It's not just the side-to-side motion of the boat that's making him sick.

Jamie doesn't know what to say, and he doesn't have to say anything. Eric gives a tight smile like he knows what Jamie is thinking. The smile of a man who just convinced someone to keep a terrible secret.

When they were kids, their dad told them:

No matter what you get into, you get the other out of it. If one of you gets in a fight, the other gets in it too. You're not one, you're two. Together, always.

No matter what, you bleed for each other, because that's what brothers do.

Matty stands at the back, watching the trail of churned water stretching out behind them, lights on the shore getting smaller and smaller. Then he turns and passes the brothers, his head hung, shoulders slumped, and goes into the galley.

Eric stands and waves for Jamie to follow him. "Come here. I want to show you something."

Jamie walks behind his brother, past the wheelhouse to the front deck. The engine drones steadily, shuddering through the entire boat like it's a living thing. The bow rises up and down in gentle degrees on the water.

"It's not always this calm," Eric says. "Sometimes it takes all you have just to keep your balance."

With his stomach against the guardrail, he leans over the bow, then looks back and smiles. "Try it."

Jamie stands beside him and does the same.

"Now, look up," Eric says.

With his upper body extended out over the water, it's as if the boat has disappeared and he's flying over the rippled surface, cool wind hissing over small cuts on his skin he didn't even know were there.

He looks over at his brother, a slight smile on his face. All those creases from earlier have smoothed out and he looks so much younger, closer to the version that exists only in Jamie's memory. The brother, friend, protector he used to have before things went bad.

Together, they fly over the ocean. Water sprays on Jamie's face and he feels the stickiness of salt.

A moment disconnected from all the moments that preceded it.

"This was on my list," Eric says.

"What was?"

Eric waves a hand at the sky, the ocean.

To hear him say he had a "list" makes Jamie feel something. A reminder of who they used to be.

"I wanted you to see this," Eric says. "It's hard to explain what it looks like once you get past all the light pollution. But once you're here, it all makes sense."

Jamie looks up and almost can't believe how many pinpoints of light dot the black sky. Millions of them, scattered like radioactive grains of sand across a black canvas. Millions are clustered together in streaks. There's something familiar about the constellations, an itch at the back of his mind that he recognizes them somehow. He can actually sense the curve of the earth in how they're stretched out. He's never been so aware of the fact they are on a planet, a sphere in space.

He heard it called "fabric" once. The fabric of space and time. As though the two things were intertwined, inseparable. Looking now at all the stars, he doesn't think of space as something above them any longer. He thinks of it being all around their spinning rock. Something they're *inside*.

Eric brings himself back over the railing and stretches. Jamie stays where he is, thinking, if he can just keep flying over the water, maybe when he comes back down there will no longer be a body in the freezer and the events of the night will have been erased, buried in the ocean.

Jamie lets the illusion last just a little longer, then grips the railing and lowers himself back down. He's about to say something to Eric when he notices Ed through the wheelhouse window, waving for them to join him in the galley.

Jamie takes one last look at the horizon, at the dark blue sky fading into black space, and he can understand how people once believed there was an edge to the world. A place where the waves flowed off a sharp surface, turning to ice in the void.

7

In the galley, Matty sits at the small table with both hands around an open can of beer. He stares vacantly as Ed finishes looping a piece of rope around the wheel to keep it straight and comes into the galley.

He gestures to the bench around the table, and both Eric and Jamie slide in next to Matty. Ed remains standing. He's slipped on a new flannel, this one yellow. He folds his arms over his broad chest and leans against the counter. The lines in his forehead, around his eyes, make Jamie think of how stone gets shaped by weather, and he wonders if years of wind and waves have etched those lines into Ed's skin.

"Listen," the captain says, his voice a deep growl. "We don't want to talk about this, but we have to. Just once." He runs his fingers over his beard, eyes moving from one man to the next.

"We're going to keep on going for another hour," he says, "then we're going to dump the body. I don't have anything on board to weigh it down, which means…"

He clears his throat, "…we'll have to cut it up."

Matty makes a burping sound, and his cheeks puff out. His skin goes pale.

Ed watches his son carefully, eyes narrowing, and says, "I've got a hacksaw…"

Matty jumps up, rushes to the sink, and retches into it. Liquid splashes, followed by the smell of bile and beer. He spits a couple of times, then lifts the cooler lid and grabs another beer. He goes back to his seat, looking like he's about to pass out, and cracks open the can.

Ed's arm swipes out so fast Jamie thinks he's going to hit his son, but his hand comes away with the can of beer crushed in his large fingers. Beer shoots out in a foamy spray, raining down on Matty's hair, his face. Ed throws the can into the sink so hard it clangs against the metal and bounces back out, splashing beer across the window.

He jabs a finger at Matty, "You *should* feel sick. There's a dead man in the hold of my ship and it's your fuckin' problem. You don't get to numb yourself from this. Not yet. We deal with it first."

Ed calms his voice, but he's still breathing hard.

"We don't want the body washing back up to shore in one piece," he says. "So, we cut it up, let the fish do the rest."

"Shit, Dad," Matty says, "do we have to…"

"This is not a fuckin' debate," Ed growls, "and we are not taking a vote. This is the plan."

He aims his finger at Eric. "And when the time comes, you're cutting the body."

Whatever Jamie saw in his brother a few minutes ago is gone now, and the muscles in his jaw are so tight they bulge under the skin.

Ed turns and goes back into the wheelhouse, aims the boat straight into the white beam that shines down from the moon and reflects off the water.

Eric pushes against Jamie until he moves, then gets up and goes outside. Matty holds his head in both hands, fingers gripping his skull. He mutters something Jamie can't hear.

Jamie finds Eric sitting on the freezer, watching the water churn behind the boat, stretching into the distance like a white carpet on a black stage. He knows better than to say anything. He sits next to his brother in silence. The lights of Waikiki are now as small and dim as stars, and they both sit in silence until they disappear.

The motion of the boat and drone of the engine lull Jamie into a sort of trance. He starts thinking about timelines and trajectories, how one small event (small in the sense it can take only seconds to occur) and the previously known path is suddenly erased.

A car crash, a pregnancy, an arrest, a fistfight.

All the events that waited for you down the line are now different. The job you'd get, the girl you'd marry, the places you'd vacation… all of that gone, replaced with an alternate version of your own life. And the crazy thing is, you don't even know what those things would have been. All you know is that it's different now, and you can feel that difference in every single shitty thing that happens. It eats away at you until you either accept this version of events, or you somehow try and get things back on track.

Is that what Dad did? Jamie wonders.

Was all the violence and the cheating just a way of kicking against a life he never wanted? Lashing out at the people around him, like maybe breaking them would make them fit better into the mold of something he actually wanted?

The sound of the engine lowers, then rumbles to a stop. Jamie stands and turns in a full circle. Ocean all around. The dark motion of water in every direction. He feels a sudden panic at the realization there is nowhere to swim to if the boat sank. Nothing but endless depth beneath him.

Water laps against the side of the boat as it rocks back and forth, and Jamie feels it in his head. A strange sort of dizziness that makes him nauseous. But there's something else, too. A pressure that surrounds him, pushing on his body, making the air feel thick, difficult to move through.

Eric rises from the freezer, rolling his shoulders, lifting each knee up high, as though he's preparing for a fight, or a marathon. He avoids eye contact with Jamie.

Voices come from the galley, first Matty (saying something about how sick he feels) then Ed (telling his son to man up and stop being a whiny bitch). Matty comes stumbling out moments later, looking like he'd throw up again if he had anything left inside him, followed by Ed who holds something in one hand.

Eric turns around, sees Ed, and takes a deep breath.

Without saying a word, Ed holds out the object in his hand. Moonlight burns along the metal of one serrated edge, and Jamie's stomach churns when he realizes it's a hacksaw.

Matty groans and pushes the heel of his hand to his right eye, staggering around the wheelhouse to the front of the boat.

"Matthew," Ed yells. "Get your ass over here."

Matty either doesn't hear, or doesn't listen, because he keeps on moving.

Jamie instinctively backs away from the freezer as Ed pops the hatch and lifts the lid with a metallic screech. Eric's hands open and close. Open and close. Jamie remembers Eric doing that exact same thing with his hands one fateful night after a high school basketball game. Waiting to jump a guy he thought had been flirting with his then-girlfriend.

Open and close in anticipation of something.

Eric beat the guy up so bad he ended up in the hospital and the cops were called. Eric was arrested, placed on probation, and given community service.

The fingers spread out wide, then close into a white-knuckled fist.

The light flickers on and ice glistens with an eerie red glow from the hold.

"Do it down there," Ed says to Eric. "I'll rinse it all out and dump the bilge when we're done."

Eric nods, his face grim. He looks at the saw in his hand, and his eyes widen for a second, as if he doesn't remember taking it from the captain.

"Matthew!" Ed yells again.

Jamie keeps backing up until he bumps into the side of the boat. From here he can see Matty standing at the bow, looking out at the water. His head tilts a little one way, then the other. He holds one arm to his stomach, like that'll help the acid boiling in his guts.

Without turning his head, Matty yells back, "Dad!"

Ed snarls a curse and leans around the wheelhouse just as Matty's voice yells again, this time with fear.

"Dad, come here!"

Ed slams the freezer hatch and runs over to his son. Matty lifts one hand and points ahead at the water. Jamie and Eric look at each other, then Eric drops the saw on the hatch and heads to the front. Jamie moves to follow and gets that feeling again that the air is pushing against him, and his limbs are heavier, like walking through water.

When he reaches the bow, the three other men are all staring out at the ocean in silence. Jamie is about to ask what they're looking at when he touches the railing and feels it vibrating against his palm. He feels it in his feet, too. He follows Matty's outstretched hand with his eyes and sees a hole in the ocean.

8

Jamie closes his eyes in one long, hard blink. When he opens them again, the hole is still there.

Black, the color of space without stars. A hundred yards in front of the boat, a perfect circle in the ocean. Not on the ocean, *in* it. The edges are white where water flows down into the chasm.

It's too far away to tell exactly how big it is, but if Jamie had to guess he'd say as long as eight *Full Speed Eds* in a row, front to back.

Matty says, "What is it?" just as Jamie notices the boat is no longer rocking from side to side. It's dipping up and down, like it did when the engine was on.

Ed's mouth hangs open, his neck craned forward. He says, "What the hell?" under his breath.

Still holding the railing, Jamie leans over the side and sees water breaking in a straight line along the hull.

Up and down. Up and down.

Pressure again. Stronger now. Pushing on his chest, against his ribcage.

"We're moving," he says, and his voice seems to drain out of him slowly, like a cassette player with dying batteries.

Ed rushes over to where Jamie is and looks down as waves flow toward the dark circle, the swells rolling straight to the edge and falling in with the sound of a quiet waterfall.

Or is Jamie imaging that sound because he thinks it should be there?

He closes his eyes and listens. He hears water all around him. It's static, white noise. More a feeling than an actual sound, but he does hear the ocean touching the boat. Lapping against it, flowing underneath it, and that's more the sound of the boat than the ocean, though. Isn't it?

Shouldn't they hear water falling off the edge?

"Shit," Ed says quietly. Then louder, "Shit."

The ocean all around the hole is a deep, dark blue, but the circle itself is completely black. It makes Jamie think of videos he's seen of sinkholes. A chasm in the earth that breaks open and swallows cars without warning. But those are always asymmetrical, jagged, like the ground has cracked.

This is perfectly round.

Matty walks backward until he bumps into the wheelhouse, and he stands there frozen, staring, chest heaving in and out.

Eric stands at the very front of the boat. His hair blows in a faint breeze. Strands of it stretch toward the hole, which means the breeze, the pull is coming from the circle.

Jamie, Matty, and Ed all backed away when they first saw that dark circle, as if a few feet of deck could somehow protect them. Eric, though, pressed his body to the railing and peered out at the anomaly. Matty and Ed both had looks of fear, and Jamie can feel the fear on his own face. The way the skin between his eyes folds is giving him a headache. There's nothing like that on Eric's face. Looking at him now, Jamie sees disbelief, maybe even surprise. But more than anything he sees fascination. Like he not only wants to see what's creating that massive hole, he wants to get closer.

Ed suddenly grabs Jamie's arm, fingers digging into his bicep, and says, "The body."

He lets go before Jamie can respond and goes over to Eric, thumps his arm with the back of a hand. "We gotta dump it now and get the fuck outta here."

Eric doesn't respond. He just stares straight ahead with his mouth open.

"Fletcher!" Ed yells.

Eric blinks and shakes his head, turns to Ed.

"The body," Ed says again, and this time Eric nods.

As they all head to the back of the boat, Jamie wants to ask his brother if he's okay because he seems off, not quite connected to what's happening.

Ed throws open the freezer lid and points down into the hold.

"Eric, Matty, jump down and hand the body up to us."

Matty opens his mouth and starts to stutter something. Ed cuts him off.

"I swear to God, kid…"

His teeth clench. He swings his head side to side once and points again.

"Get down there."

Matty looks like he wants to cry as he steps onto the ladder and lowers himself down into the freezer. Eric still hasn't said a single word. He silently follows Matty.

A.J.'s body lies half covered in ice at the bottom and Jamie wishes the man's eyes were closed. Small crystals have formed on the eyelashes, making him look like someone was dolling him up in gaudy makeup right before, or after, he was killed.

Ed looks at Jamie and says, "Right over, okay? The second we have him, right over the edge."

Down in the hold, Matty slips on the ice as he struggles to get a grip on the body's shoulders and pull it upright. Eric squats down and pushes until A.J.'s corpse is on its knees, head bowed as if in prayer.

The two men drag the body to the ladder, where Eric drapes A.J. over his back and begins climbing. Matty pushes up on the legs from below.

As soon as the body's arms come out of the hold, Ed grabs one while Jamie gets the other. The skin is cold and firm. Pieces of ice glisten like glass in the wet hair. Crystals shine around the edge of the open throat like a gruesome necklace. Ed adjusts his grip to support the torso while Jamie pulls the legs through, until they hold the body horizontally.

Ed rips off the flannel shirt he'd put on A.J. to hide the blood, throws it into the galley, then gives a nod, and they shuffle across the deck to the railing. Jamie plants his feet and they swing the body back once, then over the railing. The corpse tumbles into the dark, arms flailing, and splashes into the water. The pale face bobs above the surface, the open eyes staring straight up into the sky.

Jamie watches as the body moves with the current, slowly being pulled away from the boat, toward the hole.

Ed's shoulders sag and he lets out a long exhale, as if relieved to finally have the dead man off his ship. The body, and any connections that might lead back to his son, are now floating away toward a chasm in the ocean. Maybe the body will disappear for good into that black circle and they'll never have to worry about pieces of it washing ashore.

Ed watches the body for a few seconds, and for the first time Jamie doesn't see him as just a rough, bear of a man whose job is dragging fish up out of the ocean and gutting them on his boat. He sees him as a man trying to protect the only thing in the world that has any meaning for him. His son.

Ed looks up, beyond the body to the hole and his mouth falls open. It's so much closer now. So much larger. He makes a fist and bangs it on the railing, once, then goes over to the hold and shouts down. "Let's go boys. Get the fuck outta here."

Jamie waits at the hold and gives Eric a hand to help pull him out, then Matty. Ed goes into the wheelhouse as the bow of the boat points up at the sky, then the water.

The three men on deck bend their knees and move with the motion of the boat as it rides the swells, pulled closer and closer to the circle.

Jamie feels a vibration in his throat, like being too close to the speakers at a concert, only moments before he hears a distorted ripping echo across the sky.

The others hear it too, and Ed comes running out of the wheelhouse, looking in the direction of the hole. But it's not the hole making the sound. The ripping grows louder, like a long, thick piece of fabric being torn right down the middle.

Jamie goes to the right side of the boat and squints into the sky. The sound seems louder over here. Something coming in their direction.

Eric says, "Ed, we're moving faster."

He's right. The bow dips and rises. Jamie's stomach lifts and then drops like when an elevator catches between floors.

There's something in the sky, a black arrowhead streaking beneath the rippling clouds, a bright orange flame burning behind it.

"A jet," Jamie says.

The others turn in his direction and look into the sky. A lone plane, tearing across the night, straight toward them.

9

Ed yells, "Fuck!" then runs into the wheelhouse, and seconds later the engine rumbles under their feet. The whole boat turns to the left and the growing swells hit them broadside. The ship tilts so far that Matty's legs slam into the freezer and he falls over. Jamie grabs the railing to keep his balance as water sprays over the side and soaks him. The boat tilts the other direction and Matty rolls across the deck.

After several more waves, Ed manages to point the ship around and pushes the throttle forward. The whine of the engine is drowned out by the jet, flying so much lower than any plane Jamie has ever seen. The pilot has to see the fishing vessel, tossed on the waves.

"Shit," Eric says. "They found us."

"I don't think it's here for us," Jamie says, and points at the dark circle. "It's looking for that."

For a moment, Eric's face says he doesn't believe him. They just dumped a dead body in the water, and now this jet is flying right toward them. But Jamie is thinking, *wouldn't they send the Coast Guard? Not a jet.*

Matty struggles to his feet, a look of pure panic etched on his face, watching the plane streaking closer and closer. With one hand on the railing, Jamie makes his way to the very back, keeping an eye on the plane flying just under the clouds. The ripping sound fills his head, shredding his thoughts.

Ahead of the boat, the ocean is calm, almost glassy. But a hundred yards out from the hole the sea is being pulled backward, sucked into the gaping chasm, and Jamie can't help but picture water circling the drain in a bathtub. He feels the engine push as hard as it can. Ed's face is strained, his jaw tightened as he struggles to hold the wheel straight. No matter how hard the engine goes, the hole is pulling them toward it.

Eric joins Jamie at the back, his whole body moving with the lift and fall of the boat.

"It's going to fly right over it," he says.

Matty is on all fours, crawling toward them.

The arrowhead of the jet, such a small thing making such a big sound, is almost on top of the hole when the tail suddenly flips up, as if snatched by a giant, invisible hand, and the entire plane rises into the air along a curved arc. No longer flying, the plane is caught in the grip of something it can't escape. Metal screeches as the wings tear loose and spin off into darkness. The jet keeps rising, flames bursting from the sides until it's completely vertical above the hole. Jamie thinks of the half-circle and needle of a speedometer. The plane is the needle, and it keeps moving along the arc, upside down now, falling to the other side of the hole, scattering pieces of itself the whole way down.

It slams into the ocean and bursts apart like the dark water is concrete, scattering flaming debris over the surface of the water. A burning oil slick, and hundreds of shining metallic pieces begin immediately sliding backwards and over the edge of the hole.

Ed, still gripping the wheel, is looking back through the wheelhouse and watching the whole thing, his eyes open so wide they look like they'll fall right out of the sockets.

Matty, still on all fours, stares at the dark hole, his mouth hanging open, helpless fear on his face.

Eric holds the railing with both hands. He looks oddly peaceful and Jamie thinks he must be in shock.

He touches his brother's shoulder, says his name.

Eric doesn't look at him, he just says, "So, this is how it happens."

Jamie wants to ask what he means, but he can't breathe. He tries, but the air just wheezes through his constricted windpipe, it won't reach his lungs, and his heart pumps big and heavy. His brain struggles to make sense of what he just saw. There's no context, no precedent for it. That jet looked like it was snatched in mid-air by the hand of God and flung over the top of this dark, swirling hole at the center of the ocean.

There's a fearful beauty to the anomaly. Ringed white by the water that churns over the edge and falls into oblivion. This deep, smooth blackness against the movement of the ocean. It has dimension, even though Jamie can't make sense of that either, and he only knows this because water, and now debris, are falling into it and disappearing.

It grows larger as they get closer.

Ed yells from the wheelhouse, his gruff voice strained like he's lifting something heavy. There's a loud pop and the engine shudders, then stops. Smoke billows from the galley, from the hatch that leads to the engine room, and fills the wheelhouse. Ed starts coughing, and a second later comes running out of the wheelhouse, holding his shirt over his face. He takes one look at the hole, and goes straight to his crawling son, kneels beside him, puts his arms around Matty's neck, and pulls him close.

Without the engine, the ship glides faster toward the hole. So close now it fills Jamie's field of vision. He's not sure if it's the smoke in his eyes, but the air above the hole looks warped.

The roar of rushing water fills his ears.

He hopes it's a long fall once they hurtle over the edge. Long enough to say a prayer, to ask for forgiveness. He hopes it doesn't hurt.

Jamie grabs Eric's arms, looks into his brother's face, and sees none of his own fear. Fear so powerful it's like fire running through his blood, burning every inch of him from the inside out.

Pressure builds in his head, so intense he's afraid his eardrums will burst at any moment. His body screams, too, like his skeleton, organs, and muscles have turned to iron and are crushing him from the inside. The suffocating pressure of being dragged deep by an undertow. He expects to hear the wet, muted sound of his bones fracturing, then snapping in half. His lungs won't fill. The air all around him is thick.

The pressure has a sound, or a sound is creating the pressure — Jamie can't tell which — the harsh droning of an electric sander against a thick piece of metal. It hums along his jaw, rattles his teeth so hard it feels like they're about to slip out of his gums.

The ship bucks against the waves. The aft end lifts into the air and all Jamie sees is black sky and white stars, but distorted—the light of the stars stretches out and curves—then the boat hurtles backward and they're pointed down at the water, at the dark hole so close it fills Jamie's vision. An open mouth swallowing the ocean.

His brain is a machine throwing sparks, trying desperately to think of a way out of the situation. There's nothing to compare this event to, nothing to look at and say, *This is how we survive.* If it was just a shipwreck, you'd cling to the wreckage and pray for someone to find you. But, as far as Jamie knows, there's never been a hole in the ocean into which things disappeared.

Will anyone ever find us?

The thought terrifies Jamie. If he's never found, will Dylan think his dad walked out on him? Will Sylvia?

The water is white and frothy at the edge of the hole, whipped in a fury as it flows into the abyss. Something glistens in the air along the edge, something that catches the moonlight. Then Jamie notices the water at the edge, how most of it pours out of sight, but some of that white froth curves upward and disintegrates as it rises into the air.

While trying to keep his balance, Jamie looks up and the air all around the edge of the hole is filled with tiny orbs that sparkle like diamonds. Individual, atomized drops of water, flowing up as if on a chain. Millions and millions of them, creating something like a curtain, or chainmail made of liquid.

He doesn't know how he missed it before, but he sees it now and it's beautiful and terrifying all at once. This misty wall goes up at least a hundred feet, if not more, before curving over the top of the hole, like a bell.

The boat lifts and drops again, and Jamie's stomach goes with it. The pressure shoves air into his lungs and sucks it right back out in a painful wheeze. The stern crashes into the water forcefully and Jamie swears he feels the hull crack like they've just smashed onto a rock.

The edge is so close Jamie could stand on the railing and jump into the chasm. He thinks they should all run to the front of the boat, as far away from the hole as they can get, but it doesn't matter. Front. Back.

The whole boat is going in anyway.

He feels the pull of the water beneath them. It's not that the ship is going backward, it's the ocean, and they're carried along with it. Like when they were kids and they took the blanket off the bed and spread it on the floor. Jamie sat on it because he was the smallest, and Eric gathered up the end and pulled his little brother around the house. Jamie gripped handfuls of the sheet to keep his balance as the homemade chariot swung around corners and crashed into walls.

Eric.

He's still gazing into the abyss, lips parted, eyebrows raised. An expression, Jamie thinks, of curiosity, or controlled excitement, and he hates that it reminds him of the way he stood in front of Sleep Eric and his brother looked right through him as if he were a transparent ghost. One of Eric's hands moves to the back of his neck and rubs at the same spot he used to say "ached" back when he was laid up in bed with a fever after a night of sleepwalking.

If Eric has any of the emotions the others felt, he's already burned them and moved beyond fear into acceptance. The situation can't be changed, so he faces it straight on. Jamie can't tell if his brother is brave, enlightened, or if his brain has just completely malfunctioned due to shock.

Eric glances over, catches his brother looking at him. He gives a slight smile and says, "I always wondered when—"

The rest of his words get cut off when the back end of the boat crosses through that misty wall of water droplets floating up into the air. It passes over Jamie's face, a gentle mist, warmer than he expected, then the deck shifts under his feet. Ed yells something Jamie can't hear over the sudden roar that fills his head.

A quiet roar.

Like the sound you hear underwater. Deep, muffled static, muted by blood and pressure.

Ed keeps one arm wrapped around Matty, crushing his son against his chest, as the other hand reaches for something to grab onto. Something to keep them from sliding across the deck.

The end of the boat tips down until all Jamie sees is pure black. A black that seems to swirl and move. Inky waves that undulate with such subtlety he's not even sure it's really happening.

His shoes squeak as the deck tilts further and his stomach lurches. He grabs the railing and his body goes nearly horizontal as the boat slips further into the hole. He knows there are only seconds before the whole ship slides right off the edge.

A thought burns through his subconscious, leaving a tracer like a bullet fired at night.

How long will we fall? And will we know it when the fall ends?

Eric has both feet flat against the side, both hands on the railing. He looks down into the hole, then up to the dome of water droplets. The way he's positioned, once the boat tips over the edge, Eric will be the first to fall off. Followed by Jamie, then Matty and Ed. Four bodies will soar through the darkness as a twenty-seven-foot tuna boat chases them down to the bottom of the world.

Another thought fires…

Will we smash through to the other side?

Jamie looks behind him as the front end of the boat rises up into the air.

Any second now.

He thinks of Dylan, of Sylvie, and is paralyzed by how heavy his regrets are. Just one more hour, one more phone call and maybe he could make everything right.

His heart hammers so fast he's amazed he doesn't lose consciousness. He wants to say something, to yell at his brother and tell him he loves him one last time before they die. Tell him he wished he knew how to help him, but he didn't even know how to help himself. He wants to say he always felt sick that Eric got the worst of it from Dad. That Eric was the one Dad punished the most, and that has to affected your whole life, surely?

Maybe the way you were, the way you are, is all because of him.

I knew you were broken, he wants to say. *I knew it the whole time.*

But these thoughts exist inside that deep static, and none of them find their way to his mouth. He yells out just to hear something, and it evaporates as soon as it leaves his mouth.

The boat tips further and slides forward. Jamie's stomach lifts like at the top of a rollercoaster right before it shoots down the tracks. Eric peers into the dark like he expects to see something lurking inside it, floating up out of the black swirls.

Jamie's heart shoots up into his throat and pulses as the ship slides even more, and now there's no water underneath the back of the boat. The front end is pointed straight up at the sky. Ed loses his grip, and he and Matty fall, crash into the freezer hatch and cling there. Ed's mouth is wide open in a scream. Matty's eyes are clenched so tight they look like deep wrinkles.

This is it, Jamie thinks. *The end.*

And the boat slips over the edge.

SUSPENSION

10

Falling.

Weightless.

Jamie's body leaves the deck. He still holds the slick railing with one hand as his legs float up. Eric has let go completely, and his body is suspended against the blackness of the hole, hanging in nothing. The ship is completely vertical, falling into the abyss like a knife.

Ed's mouth remains open, screaming, but Jamie can't hear it. He can't hear anything. He thinks if he can just hold onto the railing, maybe he'll be okay.

Time seems to slow down and stretch out as they fall. Jamie is aware of so many things all at once. The three men around him. The creak and bend of the ship as it leaves the water and plummets into the darkness. A long inhale that tastes of salt-filled air, the burn as it hits his lungs.

The deep silence of the hole makes him feel as though he's falling in a dream, and he hopes that he'll wake up when he dies.

And there's Eric. Suspended in the air, arms stretched out, legs twisted, the fabric of his shirt moving like a flag, rippling slowly. His arms windmill like he's trying to right himself, to find balance, and it makes Jamie sick how long he has to watch his brother flail, knowing there's nothing he can do. At any moment, Eric will plunge into that darkness and disappear, and the rest of them will follow.

Images flash through Jamie's head. A specific memory of when they were kids. Another night he woke up to his brother climbing down from the top bunk and going outside. By the time Jamie got up and followed him, Eric had already started climbing the big maple tree in their front yard. A tree they'd both scaled a million times, but never asleep, never in this hypnotic state of disconnected movement.

Jamie hiss-whispered loud for him to come down, but Eric didn't listen. Asleep, he climbed as well as he did awake, maybe even better, and before long he disappeared into the dark canopy of leaves. Jamie walked backward until he could see the whole tree. He waited, sweating nervously, for the crack of a branch followed by Eric's body ragdoll-crashing and folding over every limb on the way down. There was a thinned-out space near the top of the tree where the power company chain-sawed a few branches that got caught in the powerlines. Jamie saw Eric's outline, his silhouette, appear in that space as he held onto a thick branch with one hand, and leaned his body out, head tilted up at the night sky. He looked like a sailor at the top of a mast in one of those old adventure movies Dad liked to watch. Jamie had no idea what his brother was looking at, but Eric stayed there in the tree for nearly an hour, like he was waiting for something, and he only came down out of the tree when he finally realized it wasn't going to happen. He marched back to the house, back to their room, got in the top bunk, dirty feet and all, and stayed there until the morning.

Jamie watches his brother's outline now, again, and it's what he feared when Eric was at the top of the tree. A freefall.

Another sound intrudes upon the muted static that fills Jamie's head. Almost like a foghorn, but bigger, deeper. The sound of something large and powerful, the deep bass of it makes his breathing shake, makes his eyes quiver in their sockets. A blast of sound so massive Jamie thinks it's going to crush him. He looks at his arm still gripping the railing and all the hair has gone stiff.

Another blast and the sound pushes on his chest, makes his heart skip beats, like he's inside the world's largest bell and it just got hammered by a mallet the size of a skyscraper.

Two pops go off in his head, one after the other, bright and painful, and he feels cold air blow deeper into his ears than it should. Hot blood pools in the canals, filling his head with the gurgle of liquid, before running down the side of his face. The force of the sound is so painful tears stream from his eyes. It feels like everything inside him is being crushed.

He tries to hold onto the railing, but his fingers slip one by one, until he's suspended like Eric, floating in oblivion. He has just enough time to look down and see Ed and Matty lifting up off the boat into the air.

There is one final blast that squeezes all the air from Jamie's lungs, and suddenly the boat levels out, as though caught by an invisible hand, and all four men come crashing down. Jamie's head slams onto the deck. Galaxies explode, and he loses consciousness.

11

It's quiet.

Jamie lifts his head slowly, hears the wet adhesive sound of partially dried blood separating from his skin and the red puddle on the deck. His whole-body aches and his head throbs with an erratic heartbeat.

It hurts to blink, but he does anyway and little white dandelion blossoms explode in his vision. He looks around for Eric, sees his brother crumpled up near one of the hydraulics. Motionless. Ed and Matty, too. Ed on his back, arms and legs splayed out. Matty, half on the freezer hatch, dented inward by his shoulders, arms, and face. The other half of him kneels on the deck.

Jamie struggles to his knees. He touches his head and feels around until his fingers find an open gash on his scalp. The wound burns to touch and his fingers come away slick with blood.

How am I still alive?

He walks, expecting to feel the motion of the boat beneath him, but it's perfectly stable. In fact, it doesn't seem to be moving at all. Jamie stumbles over to Eric and touches his brother's shoulder. He moans, tries to push himself up, and collapses again.

Jamie sits down next to him. "What hurts?"

Eric moans again.

"Come on, talk to me. What's hurting?"

Eric leans on one elbow and points to his ankle. Jamie gently pulls up the jeans and realizes the foot is facing the wrong way. The toes of Eric's shoes are pointed backwards, and the flesh around the ankle is purple and swollen, full of fluid. Jamie heaves and swallows back bile.

"Stay here," he says. "I'll be right back."

Jamie makes his way across the deck to the galley, stopping only to make sure Ed and Matty are both breathing—he'll take care of them in a minute. Cold droplets of water fall off Jamie's face, splash onto the deck.

Shit, it's going to rain.

When he gets inside the galley, he digs through the drawers looking for a Ziploc bag, but all he finds is a box of tinfoil. He rips off a long sheet, opens up the cooler, and starts scooping handfuls of ice onto the foil, then he twists it up. Already, the metallic bag is getting cold. He absently licks at some of the rain that's run over his lips, and tastes salt.

Back on the deck he finds Eric sitting up, gazing skyward. Jamie presses the foil covered ice on his brother's ankle and holds it there.

"You okay?" he asks.

Eric doesn't say anything, he just keeps looking up.

Jamie snaps his fingers twice. "Hey, Eric, look at me. Let me see your eyes. Tell me if you're okay. Are you hurting anywhere else?"

Without looking away from the sky, Eric lifts a hand and points one finger straight up. Jamie follows the direction of his brother's finger and sees dark ocean waves rolling above them.

"Is that…?"

Jamie can't think of the right words because the question he wants to ask doesn't make any sense.

Is that the ocean?

He moves Eric's hand down to the tinfoil and says, "Hold this," then gets up and stands at the edge of the railing. More raindrops fall on his face. He licks his lips again and tastes salt. Looking straight ahead, the horizon is blurry, like he's viewing it through a rain-soaked car windshield. He tilts his vision slowly until he's once again looking at the sky. A sudden feeling of vertigo spins his head and makes him nauseous.

Waves ripple along the sky. Dark water stretches in every direction, moving in exactly the same way as he'd seen when they were speeding away from the island until the ocean surrounded them. He feels that same helplessness now.

It can't be real.

He rubs at the wound on his head again, winces at the pain. Would he feel that if he were in a coma, or dead? Would his nerves spark at lacerated flesh?

Would he taste salt? And if the ocean is above them, what's below?

Jamie takes two steps back without looking. Eric keeps holding the ice to his ankle, staring up at the water with a dumb smile, like it's some kind of magic trick. Ed groans and sits up, shaking his head. When he sees Matty's body slumped over the freezer hatch, his motions become frantic. He gets to his knees and crawls over to his son, saying his name over and over.

Droplets of water ping off the hatch, gently pop on the deck. The air, the space they exist inside is so quiet it's unnerving. Jamie inches toward the railing, hunching down a little as he grabs hold, and leans his head out over the edge.

More than vertigo this time, it's a catastrophic system failure as he gazes down into a sky full of stars. Shredded clouds drift apart and reveal the dust of the Milky Way, strewn across the blackness like a fistful of sand. Those familiar constellations (even though he still can't remember why he knows them) slowly spin.

His legs go so numb he can't feel them anymore, and he falls to the deck beside Eric. Ed is still saying Matty's name, almost lying on top of his son and trying to shake him awake.

Jamie finds all the questions running through his head obvious and stupid.

What is happening?

Is this real?

Are we all dead?

At the word "dead" he glances over and hopes Matty is still alive just as the man's body jerks upright. He stumbles backward, trips over his father's leg, and falls on his ass.

Ed kneels in front of him. "Can you hear me? Matthew, do you hear my voice?"

Matty looks around confused, his eyes moving across the boat until he sees Eric and Jamie. He nods slowly and reaches up to touch a red line on his right cheek. His eyes clench shut and as he lets out a groan of pain, the red line splits apart like a second mouth. Flaps of skin dangle and Matty's teeth are visible through the sliced opening. Blood pours down his face as he howls, it fills his mouth and he spits out a bright red spray.

Jamie notices blood all over the freezer hatch and thinks Matty must have bashed his face on the lock when he fell.

Ed helps his son to his feet and guides him to the galley. Matty tries to speak and crimson liquid comes leaking out of his mouth, coating his chin like red paint.

Jamie turns his attention to Eric, says, "Come on, let's get to the galley. Maybe they have some meds in the first-aid kit."

Eric's eyes are half-closed, and they float around like he's drunk. He purses his lips and shakes his head as Jamie stands and tries to get him up. No, Eric can't walk, but maybe he can hop the fifteen feet to the galley and lie down on the bench.

Matty's continued howls come from inside, followed by Ed's gruff voice trying to sooth him.

"Come on," Jamie says, pulling on his brother's arm. "Let's get some meds and then figure this out."

Eric reluctantly rises to his one good foot, and instead of heading toward the galley, he hobbles straight for the back of the boat. Jamie rushes to his side and tries to turn him around, but he's already leaning over the boat and gazing down into the sky.

Fear grips Jamie's throat and squeezes. His fingers dig into Eric's muscle as he watches the clouds drift across stars. He's not afraid that Eric will fall overboard, no, Jamie has a tight grip on his brother's shoulder with one hand, and an equally tight grip on his arm with the other hand. So, what is he afraid of?

It comes to him suddenly and clearly.

He's terrified Eric will jump. That he'll break free of his claw-like grasp and throw himself over the edge. And if he's honest with himself, that has been a deep fear Jamie's had since after Eric started sleepwalking, after Dad left, and after Eric moved out on his own. The recklessness that became part of Eric's personality made him unable, or unwilling, to consider consequences. Too often, it was blind momentum that carried him. It's how he landed every job he ever had. How he ended up in Hawaii. Just blindly following whatever "road" he believed was opening up before him. If he wanted to do something, he usually did it.

It's why Jamie's heart suffered an electric shock every time his phone rang at night. A dark voice in the back of his head whispered, *Something bad happened to Eric. Something real bad, and you weren't there to stop him.*

Jamie never feared that Eric would fall in a depression and put a gun to his head, or purposefully OD on medication. No, he feared Eric heard a dark voice sometimes, too. A voice that told him to do bad things, and he could never tell the difference between the good voice and the bad voice.

The good voice told him to do hard things. Things that required work, patience, persistence, and self-sacrifice.

The bad voice said, stab the needle in your arm, snort the powder, hit first and hit hardest, push the pedal to the floor and outrun that other voice.

Jamie feared his brother would someday commit suicide simply because he couldn't think of a good reason not to. Because the bad voice hissed in his ear, *Do it. See what comes next. Have an adventure.*

Now, the salt Jamie tastes is from tears rolling down his face. He pulls Eric back and his brother leans forward harder.

"I want to see," he says. "I need to see it."

Heavy footsteps come across the deck, followed by Ed's voice. "Everyone okay out here?"

Jamie looks back and gives a tight smile, but Eric keeps staring down at the stars.

"I got Matt all patched up," Ed says with a smile barely seen beneath his beard. "He needs stitches though." Then he nods at Eric and says, "Everything okay?"

The look on Eric's face, Jamie can only describe it as "awe." Like the danger, or weirdness, or straight-up horror of the situation is completely lost on him. All he sees is this magnificent impossibility. A ship sailing through the clouds. Even Ed seems too cheerful, too oblivious.

Am I the only one thinking clearly? Jamie wonders.

Maybe the others hit their heads hard. Really hard. Maybe Jamie did too, but everything feels real and he's as terrified as he thinks everyone else should be.

He gestures to the railing. "You need to take a look, Ed."

Ed's smile wavers as he comes closer. His eyes narrow, distrustful, like Jamie is playing a trick. He looks at Eric, says his name, and Eric doesn't move. Ed stands beside Jamie, looks him up and down, then leans over the edge. For a few seconds, all Jamie can hear is his breathing getting faster and faster, a whistle and wheeze from his nose. Then his head starts shaking back and forth. He backs away quickly, still shaking his head, and whispers, "Jesus Christ almighty.

He keeps walking backwards until his calves hit the freezer hatch. "Jesus Christ almighty," he screams.

Both hands clamp over his head as he turns in a complete circle, like he's looking for something to fix a situation that can't be fixed.

It's Ed's screaming that gets Eric to finally turn around. His eyes have a glassy look. He blinks slowly and hops toward the captain with Jamie hurrying alongside to help keep him upright.

More rain falls, and it feels thicker to Jamie than normal water. The weight as it hits his skin seems heavier.

Ed grabs handfuls of his own hair and pulls. His untucked flannel is torn and stained with blood. He paces back and forth like a caged animal, huffing through his nose. Eric puts a hand on the captain's arm and points up. Ed looks and his mouth instantly falls open. His eyes widen.

"What the hell is going on?" He wheezes.

Matty appears in the galley doorway, leaning against the frame with a red-soaked piece of gauze taped over his cheek. He steps out, gazes up at the sky and lets out a laugh, even though his face is pale and horrified. Rain continues to fall, illuminated by the spotlight of a moon somewhere underneath the boat. The drops sparkle and spin, and Matty closes his eyes, opens his mouth, and lets those small pearls of water land on his tongue. Jamie wonders if he can taste the salt.

He laughs again. "Upside down," he says. "Upside fucking down."

12

They gather in the galley. Jamie and Matty on the inside of the table, Eric on the outside so he can stretch out his leg and rest it on the cooler. Jamie checked the ankle again before replacing the melted ice in the tinfoil, and the bruise had spread, the colors grown deeper shades of purple and blue, like the sky before a storm. He found some Tylenol and ibuprofen in the first-aid kit and gave Eric three of each.

Ed sits at the other end of the table until he can't sit any longer, then he stands and leans against the sink, arms folded over his chest. One hand occasionally lifting to rub at his beard with a sound like sandpaper.

The creases in his forehead, between his eyes, have not unfolded since he saw the ocean above their heads. Rain patters down on the roof, pings off the freezer and railing. Beyond that, out in the space they float through, it is quiet. Sometimes Jamie thinks he hears something distant, a low humming, but he can't be sure that isn't the result of cracking his skull on the deck.

"Okay," Ed says, looking at the floor. "I want everyone to say their full names. Also… where you were born. Eric, you first."

Eric is looking through the door to the strangely shimmering air beyond the black space.

"Eric?"

His eyes remain fixed, and he says slowly, "Eric Dylan Fletcher. Ashland, Oregon."

Jamie is next in line, so he says, "James Ethan Fletcher. Ashland, Oregon."

Matty picks at a gouge in the table-finish with his fingernail. A clicking sound, every time. The gauze on his face blooms with fresh red wetness when he says, "Matthew Michael Clanahan. Pocatello, Idaho."

Ed still has one hand in his beard, stroking over and over, and his voice comes from between his fingers. "Edward Harrison Clanahan. Cleveland, Ohio."

He stares straight ahead while he says it, then his eyes fall to the watch on his wrist. He stops scratching and lifts the arm up.

"Shit. My watch is stopped. Any of you wearing one?"

Jamie pulls back his sleeve to reveal the cheap watch he bought at a gas station since he's not allowed to keep a phone in his pocket on the job. He started wearing it on the inside of his wrist because he was told that was a faster way to check the time, and you were less likely to bang the face of it while working. After wearing it for a few weeks, he stopped taking it off when he got home and found he preferred checking the watch to digging a phone out of his pants whenever he wanted to know the time.

It's an analog watch because he always liked watching the secondhand tick across the numbers. Like he could actually see time moving.

Jamie holds up his hand. "Stopped at 2:27 a.m."

Ed's eyes widen a little. "Mine too."

He disappears into the wheelhouse for a moment, then comes back out shaking his head. "Clock in there's dead too. Same time."

Matty digs into the pocket of his shorts and takes out his cellphone. The screen is dark and it won't turn on. Jamie tries his phone with the same results.

Ed returns to his place in front of the sink, the features visible above his beard all so creased Jamie can almost imagine the gears turning in his head. Heavy, metal grooves connecting, twisting with such force it's painful. Trying so hard to come up with an answer that doesn't require tiptoeing into the unnatural.

"Alright, listen," Ed says. "Something's happening here, clearly. We're caught in a weather event that—"

"Weather event?" Matty says. There's scorn in his voice. "A fucking weather event? Jesus, Dad."

Ed's eyes flash wide and he points a finger. "Careful, son. Remember who you're talking to."

Matty's voice goes higher. "This isn't fucking *Wizard of Oz*, pops. We're not in a tornado."

In spite of Ed's anger, he seems to realize that his suggestion of a "weather event" doesn't make sense. There'd be far more chaos if they were lifted up and spinning at the center of a storm. If anything, it's unnaturally calm and quiet.

"Okay, okay," Ed says, waving one hand, "a sinkhole then. Maybe some kind of geological formation we've never seen before. We fall in and the gravity of the earth holds us in place."

"Gravity," Eric whispers, and Ed ignores him, or doesn't hear him say it. But Jamie does, and he watches his brother with a kind of fearful fascination.

"Are there even sinkholes in the ocean?" Matty asks.

"How the fuck should I know?" Ed shouts.

Matty stands, his gauze turning deeper shades of red with every word he says. "You're trying to say everything we already know it's not," he yells. "Storms, sinkholes, someone pulled the fucking plug on the ocean and we're just swirling around the drain. It's none of those things and you know it."

Ed takes two steps forward and jabs a meaty forefinger into Matty's chest so hard he falls back onto the bench.

"You got an explanation?" Ed says, standing over his son. "I'm trying to go through all the possibilities—"

"Not all of them," Eric says quietly.

Ed's head snaps in Eric's direction. "What was that?"

"Not all of them," he says again.

Matty exhales loudly, now that his father's anger is off him. Jamie catches his eye, gives a small nod to let him know he doesn't think he's being stupid. Jamie isn't sure it helps, but Matty nods back.

"What could do this?" Ed says. "What could keep us...suspended like this?"

Eric won't look at Ed, and Jamie gets the feeling it's not because he doesn't want to, but because he's far too interested in what's happening outside. Water keeps raining down from the ocean. It glistens on the deck, a shade that's somewhere between green and blue. It reflects the motion of the waves in the sky, making it appear alive in some way Jamie can't quite explain to himself.

The patter of rain fills the silence. Jamie notices the boat doesn't shift and creak like it did on the water. If he closes his eyes, he can easily imagine they are docked on dry land. He also doesn't feel any of the seasickness that plagued him earlier. It creates a strange sort of tension within him, the feeling of being on a boat with none of the sensations of being on a boat. Somewhere in his mind, in a place so far back he's not even sure he wants to drag it forward, is the awareness of being in the middle of the ocean, but also not. The ocean is above them, or they are above the ocean, only upside down.

Eric finally turns to face Ed and says, "A machine."

The sleeves of Ed's flannel are rolled up, revealing his hairy forearms. He smooths his mustache with thumb and forefinger, prepared to disagree with Eric, but he nods slowly, one side of his mouth curving.

"A machine?" he says. "You mean like an oil rig or something?" He nods even faster, "Right, right. An underwater oil rig. Maybe something really high-tech they've haven't told us about yet."

Eric's face has a humorless smile, and he starts to shake his head, opens his mouth to correct Ed and Jamie suddenly does not want to hear whatever he's about to say so he speaks up, "Ed, we haven't tried the engine yet. Might be worth it to see if we're able to move."

Matty snickers at the suggestion and Jamie ignores him.

"It's busted," Ed says, still watching Eric. "And we're in the fuckin' air."

"Right," Jamie says, "which doesn't make any sense. So, maybe being able to move or steer, or something, shouldn't make sense either. But maybe it does."

Ed looks at Matty, who shrugs, and lifts a hand to touch gauze on his face. His fingers come away wet with blood.

Ed stands quietly for several seconds, then lets out a sigh and says, "Fuck it. Why not?" He heads into the wheelhouse and a moment later the engine sputters a few times then rumbles to life, so much louder than it was when the blades were spinning underwater. It shakes the whole boat and Jamie smells the exhaust, hears the mechanics of the engine working hard against nothing. If he was able to see those steel turbines, he knows they'd just be spinning uselessly against the air.

Ed spins the wheel, cursing to himself as he does. The boat doesn't move at all. The engine sounds like when Jamie first learned to drive stick, when he didn't quite have the hang of clutch-shift-gas, and the awful sound of metal scraping against metal until he shoved the gearshift into place. He remembers Eric sitting in the passenger seat laughing, saying, "Grind it 'til you find it."

Once, sitting at the bar he frequented back home, a man came in and took the stool next to Jamie. He ordered a Jack and coke and rolled out a large piece of paper that looked like some kind of blueprint. Turned out, the man was a machinist making parts for a new plane Boeing was manufacturing. Every piece was separated from each other, floating in space so you could see each individual part, each gear, plate, and shaft. He told Jamie it was an "exploded view." A visual representation of the machinery pulled apart and spread out. He would machine the pieces, and Boeing would know how they were all supposed to fit together.

Jamie wishes he could have an "exploded view" of their situation so he could understand where they were, what they were inside.

What held them up?

What generated the space around them, the air in which they were suspended?

What individual pieces made this possible?

Matty lowers his head to the table and moans, "God, I'm so thirsty."

The boat engine turns off and shudders to a halt. A second later there's the sound of radio static sliding between stations. "Hello, hello," Ed says. "Anyone out there? Can anyone hear me?"

More static.

Ed flicks the radio off and yells out, "God damn it!" and hammers the palm of his hand against the wheel. He comes back into the galley, beads of sweat rolling down from his hairline.

"We're not going anywhere," he says. "Not until whatever this is lets us go."

13

Matty gets up from the bench and goes over to the cooler Eric has his leg resting on. Eric moves his leg, grimacing as he does, so Matty can take out a bottle of water and a few beers. This time, Ed doesn't say anything.

Matty hands a beer to Eric, one to Jamie, and another to his father, who cracks it open with a hiss and takes a long drink. Three more cans hiss open as Matty, Jamie, and Eric open theirs. Eric holds his can up in a salute, the others do the same, and they all drink.

Ed finishes his beer with one more long swallow, then holds the empty can to his forehead. Rolls it across his flushed skin.

"I don't know what to do," he says.

Eric runs his thumb over the aluminum can, swiping beads of moisture. "There's nothing we can do. Nothing except wait."

Jamie takes one sip of beer and sets the can down. It tastes foul, spoiled.

"Wait for what?" he asks.

Eric's eyebrows arch. "Whatever comes next."

Ed's hand tightens around his beer can and crushes it. "What the fuck does that mean?" He moves across the galley, filling the space between the table and the kitchenette. "What the fuck do you mean, 'whatever comes next?'"

For the first time since they found themselves suspended in mid-air, Eric comes out of his trance. His lips tighten and he sits up straighter, dragging his twisted ankle over the lid of the cooler. Jamie knows if he could stand on both feet, he'd be up in Ed's face in a heartbeat.

Eric slams the can on the table. Beer bubbles from the top. "Exactly what I said, Ed. Whatever comes next. Do we fall up or do we fall down? Does the ship start spinning so fast it flies apart? Or…" waving both hands down, "does the ocean come falling over us like a flood?"

Emphasizing each word, "Whatever. Comes. Next."

Ed backs up a step, his frame so much larger in the small galley, and slaps a hand to his head. He smiles crazily. "Okay, I get it now." He claps his hands together and it sounds like a gunshot. "Holy shit, man. Holy shit. I see it all. Good God almighty, I see the light!" He wags a finger in Eric's direction, "You sneaky piece of shit. This is you, isn't it? This is all you."

Matty looks at the captain, worried. "Dad, what are you talking about?"

Ed laughs in a way that twists Jamie's heart a little. The kind of laugh that usually precedes cruelty.

"Matthew," Ed says, not looking at his son, "I bet you didn't know Eric Fletcher came to me with a proposal a few weeks ago. A proposal to expand the business without you."

Matty looks from his father to Eric and back again, confusion wrinkling on his face.

"Oh yes," Ed continues, still wagging his finger. "Eric, here, said you were lazy, clumsy, a drunk, and, how did you put it Eric? Inefficient? Was that the word you used? I think it was."

Hurt takes over Matty's features. His eyes fall to the beer can clutched in his hand. He sets it on the table softly and folds his hands in his lap.

"He wanted to add another boat to the fleet, said we could double our catch. Triple it, if we got rid of you."

Jamie, stuck in the middle of the bench between Matty and Eric, says, "Ed, come on. What's the point of this? We should be trying to figure out what to do."

The large finger swings toward Jamie. "And then you show up out of nowhere," Ed says. "You meet up with my son and your brother, and then a few hours later there are two bodies in an alley."

Jamie has to look away from Ed's face because it reminds him too much of Dad. Reminds him of the way he'd get when he had too much to drink, but maybe it wasn't even the booze, maybe it was just Dad. Jamie wanted to believe he only got that angry, irrationally angry, when he was drunk, but searching through his memory Jamie isn't sure that's true. Dad's baseline was righteous anger. Whether it was about politics, his job, the city, co-workers, there was enough hate in Dad's heart to launch into a spiteful tirade about them all with hardly any provocation.

The way Ed's eyes pulse in time with his words, the way his voice has become deeper, raspier, transports Jamie right back to being a young boy in the backyard, trying to explain why there were small circular marks embedded in the fence. He and Eric had set up a target there to practice throwing darts and didn't think about what was behind it. How could Dad get so mad about something so small? Because he was a bull at the rodeo, trapped in a cage until that door opened. He wanted, needed, to thrash and kick and throw off whatever was on his back.

Ed is looking at Eric now, who returns his stare, nostrils flaring as he listens.

"You," Ed yells. "You gave A.J. the drugs. You murdered him. And you're the reason we're out here in the middle of the goddamn ocean to get rid of his corpse."

Eric starts shaking his head and he doesn't stop. He keeps saying "No" over and over, and each time it gets louder until he's shouting over Ed.

"No, Ed, no! None of this is true and you know it."

Ed slams a fist on the counter and Jamie is surprised the whole unit remains intact. "Just a few hours ago I wouldn't have believed you could kill a man," Ed yells. "Now, here we are. Everything bad that's happening is happening because of you. So, yeah, maybe you did set all this up. Maybe," pointing the finger again, "maybe you knew what was going on out here and thought you could get rid of more than one body."

The finger tremors as Ed's face grows so bright red, Jamie is amazed the man doesn't clutch his chest and fall dead.

"This is my fucking ship," he growls. "Mine."

It's pathetic, but Jamie feels like a small child caught between his parents fighting. The only person he has any sympathy for is Matty, who sits trembling silently as the two men scream at each other. Jamie thinks the only reason Ed hasn't stalked over and pummeled Eric into a bloody pulp is the broken ankle, twisted, and swollen as a dead fish.

Ed keeps on pushing his conspiracy theories, but Eric looks over at Matty and snaps his fingers. "Matty, hey. Buddy, listen to me. I never said any of those things to your dad, okay? I did suggest we add another boat. I also suggested you be on that boat with me. Ed here, he took it the wrong way. I said you'd work better with me than with him."

Matty lifts up his eyes, and they're almost as red as his father's face. He looks absolutely torn between two people he trusts. Two people he cares about. He groans, wraps both arms around his stomach, and says, "I'm so thirsty."

He opens his bottle of water, takes a drink, and makes a face like it tastes bad. He gets up and brushes past his dad, starts opening cabinets and searching until he finds a blue container of salt.

"Listen," Eric says. "You know me. I'm a fuck up and I can be selfish, but I never planned any of this."

"You're a fuckin' liar!" Ed roars, and he moves closer to the table, like he wants to stand between Eric and Matty.

Jamie watches, confused, as Matty dumps salt into his water bottle. Tiny grains spill all over the counter. He replaces the cap, shakes it until the salt dissolves and turns the water cloudy. Then he takes another drink, and continues swallowing until the bottle is empty. No one else seems to notice, but Jamie swallows and swears he can almost taste the salt—can feel it burn his tongue, choke his throat, the grit stuck between his teeth—and he can't understand why Matty would do that.

Eric lowers his voice, showing a self-control Jamie didn't know he had. "Just because shit happens doesn't mean it has to be someone's fault."

He adjusts his leg, winces his eyes shut as he grips his pant leg and shifts to a more comfortable position.

Ed gives a nasty smile and says, "Yeah, except when all the bad shit happens around one person, you gotta ask yourself why."

Eric exhales, hangs his head. "Why," he repeats. "Why."

"And another thing," Ed says. "You said something about a machine. What do you know that you're not telling us?"

As soon as the words leave Ed's mouth, something falls onto the deck outside. Jamie catches a glimpse in his periphery. A streak of white that lands on the deck with a *smack*. Matty's body jerks at the sound.

Eric looks through the door, but Ed charges out into the rain, stops where the thing fell and picks it up. He comes back inside holding up a white, low-top tennis shoe.

"What the hell is this?" He says.

Matty swallows hard, face contorted as he grips his stomach tighter. Jamie tries to think of why the shoe is so familiar.

All four of them stare at it in confusion until Eric says, "It's A.J.'s."

14

Ed holds the shoe up close to his face, like he's not sure Eric is right. Then his eyes widen and he tosses the sneaker behind him, back onto the deck. Matty groans again and says, "My stomach hurts so bad."

The captain's frame fills the entire doorway, blocking their exit outside, and Jamie wishes he had a weapon. A knife, or a gun, something to threaten the man in case he gets violent. Ed's eyes dart between Jamie and his son. Finally, his shoulders sag and he says, "I think I have something in the kit."

Matty's head almost rests on the table. Sweat rolls off his face and pools on the surface. Jamie can feel fever heat radiating off him. He hears a gurgle in the man's guts like a kid making motorboat sounds in a swimming pool.

Ed opens the first-aid kit and digs through it, dumping pill bottles, gauze, ointment and bandages into the sink until he finds a bottle of pink liquid and hands it over to his son. Matty lifts his head, unscrews the cap, and takes two long swigs. Jamie smells the medicine, can imagine its taste. Another gurgle and Matty folds, moans, and says, "This hurts so bad."

Eric's back to looking outside, at the lone shoe this time. Lying on the deck like a strange white fish.

Ed comes over and kneels in front of Eric, rests one big arm on the table and looks directly into Eric's eyes. Eric's head turns to meet his gaze.

"I'm only going to ask this once," Ed says. "Is there anything you need to tell us about what's going on?"

If his ankle wasn't broken, Jamie thinks Eric would probably be on his feet, screaming into the captain's face, if not outright trying to wrestle him to the ground. But since he's confined to sitting, Eric manages to keep his composure and says, "Everything that happened before we called you was my fault, Ed. And I'm sorry Matty and you got involved. I'm the only one who should be out here, right now."

Ed shakes his head slowly and Jamie watches the hand on the table clench into a fist. Jamie clenches his own in reaction, ready to jump up the moment Ed so much as touches Eric.

"What does that mean?" Ed says. "What do you know?"

Something heavy slams to the deck outside. There's a flash of silver in the sky, and a moment later there's another slam. And another. One after the other, these objects fall and hit the deck like bags of cement on a wet surface.

Jamie looks up to the stretch of sky between the boat and the ocean above them and sees dozens of objects falling. Some large, some small. He wonders for a second if the water raining down from the sea has frozen, and chunks of ice are bombarding the boat.

There's movement from the things hitting the deck. A spastic, frantic sort of jerking that makes the deck appear as though it's alive.

More bash onto the roof above their heads.

Bang

Bang bang bang

Jamie's shoulders twitch with each crash.

Ed stands, and with both hands against the door frame, leans outside to look up at the ocean. He jumps back as something crashes at his feet. A fish, unlike anything Jamie has ever seen, twists and trembles its way into the galley. Silver scales with thick blue and purple veins running along the sides. The fins on its back are jagged spikes, at least six inches long, and remind Jamie of those knives he's seen online. Blades forged to be as brutal and damaging as possible. Even the scales are sharp, flared out so that if anyone grabbed it their hand would be sliced to ribbons.

The fish's eyes are pure black with a thin, white vertical slit.

Ed lets out a bellow of, "What the fuck?" and backs away from the thrashing thing, its jaws opening and snapping shut with a cracking sound. Its teeth are curved with hooked barbs at each end, so big, the creature's mouth can't even close all the way. From tip to tail, the fish is as long as Jamie's arm.

Eric stares with a look of clinical detachment as the fish continues to lurch across the floor. Matty moans even louder and stands on the seat, yelling something unintelligible, arms still wrapped around his stomach. Ed lunges for the kitchen drawers, yanks one open, and shoves his hand inside. It emerges holding a rusty filet knife. He dances around, trying to avoid the whipping tail with its sharp, protruding spikes that gouge lines in the floor.

There's a wet choking sound that Jamie at first mistakes for Matty, thinking he's going to vomit, but the sound comes from the writhing creature.

Its vacant eyes stare upward, unblinking, as a wet retching (like Sylvia kneeling over the toilet in their apartment the morning after they found out she was pregnant) comes from its mouth. There's a crack and the fish's jaws unhinge, and something wriggles inside its throat.

Ed jumps forward and stomps on the creature, then leaps back with a yell. He falls against the counter, lifting his foot. Blood leaks from a hole in the sole of his shoe and drips to the floor.

"Son of a bitch!"

Worms.

That's the first thought that comes to Jamie's mind as he watches the long, thin, bone-white appendages come crawling out from between the curved teeth.

This thing swallowed a couple dozen worms and they're all caught in its throat.

A mass of writhing tentacles, smooth and colorless, emerge and begin slithering along the floor like each one has a mind of its own. It takes Jamie a moment to realize these aren't individual worms, maybe not even worms at all, but a mass of tissue connected to the creature. Part of it. Soon, they're stretched out nearly as long as the fish, all moving independently, fluttering like they're sniffing the air. They crawl toward the cooler and bend to move up the side, growing more frantic the closer they get to Eric's damaged ankle.

Jamie grabs his brother by the shoulders and pulls with all his strength, just as the worms curl around the lid and rise up like cobras about to strike.

Eric screams as his leg falls off the cooler and hits the bench, but he yanks his foot up in spite of the pain. Ed lets out a yell and comes charging over with the knife held in one fist, blade pointed down, and drives the sharp end straight into the creature's eye. Dark jelly oozes from the socket and the fish stiffens, shakes once, and stops moving. It takes another second or two for the worm-like tentacles to shiver and go still.

Leaving the knife stuck in the creature's head, Ed stands and limps to the doorway, looks out at the deck of his ship as more silvery objects smash onto it. Jamie gets up on the bench and steps over his brother to stand beside the captain.

He tries to swallow but can't.

The entire deck is covered with creatures that have rained down from the ocean above them.

15

Ed reaches a hand outside the door and grabs a two-foot pole with a curved steel hook at the end. He jabs the point into the body of the fish and drags it to the threshold, white worms trailing behind it. With a grunt, Ed lifts and tosses the creature, deftly slipping out the hook and flinging the fish onto the deck, which appears alive with the constant motion of all the creatures that cover its surface.

Jamie has never heard fish make noise before, but there's a guttural sound coming from outside, along with the wet slapping of fish thrashing out their final minutes, trying to make it back to water.

A silver rain falls from the dark hole. Small objects that spin as they tumble through space, catching and throwing the moonlight that shines from under the boat. Hundreds of them scatter over the ship, hitting the roof with small pops, pouring over the larger creatures. These smaller objects flip into the air. Clearly fish of some kind, but Jamie can't tell if they're as deadly and armored as the larger ones.

Ed stands in the doorway, silver scales and blood stuck to the end of the gaff hook, and looks at the scene with wide eyes. Then he slams the door shut and turns to the three other men. There's a confused look of terror on his face. He glances out the window of the door, watches the deck for a moment, then says, "Matt, get over here."

Matty rises from the bench with an arm still around his stomach. His skin has gone pale, and beads of sweat shine from his forehead. He joins his dad at the door.

"You recognize anything out there?" Ed says.

Matty's sweat drenched face presses against the glass, leaving a greasy streak.

Jamie watches Matty's eyes scan the deck, growing bigger with each pass. He shakes his head. Something bangs against the door, like a man's fist, and Matty jumps back, groaning as he holds his belly.

"What's the matter with you?" Ed says.

"My stomach," Matty says. "Feels like it's twisting up."

Ed nods toward the bottle on the table. "Get some more Pepto."

Matty obeys and shuffles over, grabs the bottle of pink liquid, rejoins his dad at the door and takes another long swig.

Another bang, this one louder, and Jamie pictures some large, spined fish slamming its tail against the door, more of those white worms twisting out of its mouth. Ed holds the gaff hook in both hands, like the door might suddenly burst open.

He points one finger at Jamie and motions him over, then turns his eyes to the ceiling, listening.

Jamie stands on the bench and climbs over his brother. Eric hasn't a said a word since the strange fish arrived, and he stares out the window, watching the movement and flashes of silver from the deck with an almost drugged-out expression. Jamie guesses it's probably pain. Intense pain that's shut off his other functions. He has no idea if there are any arteries running through the ankle. If so, Eric might be bleeding inside which could explain his detachment.

The thought makes Jamie's skin flush. He stands next to Ed, who whispers in his ear, "Listen. I think it's stopped."

Jamie listens, and the captain is right. There's the sound of whatever is crashing around outside the door, but it's gone quieter, and nothing else falls out of the sky.

The ocean, Jamie reminds himself. *The sky is beneath us.*

"Look at 'em," Ed whispers.

It's hard to see in the dark, so Jamie lifts part of his shirt and wipes the moisture off the door window. He can tell the deck is covered in a variety of creatures, most of them fish, although he can't recognize any of them. Many appear to be variations of the one Ed killed, but others are more bloated with big, bulging eyes. Some are long and snake-like. None of them seem to have any obvious color until moonlight, reflecting off the water above them, ripples over their scales and reveals bright veins of purple, yellow, pink, and blue.

One creature, motionless on the freezer hatch, has deep yellow eyes the color of egg yolk. It twitches randomly, its long teeth glistening.

Jamie smells the Pepto on Matty's breath as he leans forward, can smell his body odor. His eyes are wide and unblinking.

"We need to get these fuckers off my ship," Ed says. "I been on the ocean for most of my life, and I ain't never seen fish like this. I pulled up a lot of weird shit in my day, but these are something else. And I think those worms were probably some kinda parasite. Others might have it too. We gotta get rid of 'em."

Jamie nods, looks down at the floor and sees a growing puddle of blood under Ed's shoe. He wonders if the man can even feel it. And since it was pierced by that fish's spine, he also wonders if the foot will become infected.

Ed taps the window with a finger. "There's a shovel in the freezer, and—" moving his finger, "—a machete stashed on the other side. I'll give Matty the gaff hook, you get the shovel and I'll grab the machete. Matty and I'll kill as many as we can while you throw 'em off the side."

"What about Eric?" Jamie asks.

The captain looks over at him staring out the window, then back to Jamie. "Can he walk?"

"I don't think so."

"Then he stays here." He turns to Matty. "Go grab the waders."

Matty still looks like he's going to vomit any second, but he nods vigorously and heads toward the wheelhouse. He leans over, lifts a hatch in the floor, and disappears down a ladder. Jamie hasn't been down there, but he knows from phone conversations with Eric in the past that's where the crew quarters are. Right next to the engine room. Small, cramped bunks that always smell of oil and exhaust. Jamie has no idea how anyone could possibly sleep with miles of ocean pressing up against the hull only inches from your head.

A minute later, Matty comes back up the ladder carrying two rubber waders with boots attached over his shoulders. He hands one pair to his dad, along with some work gloves, and says to Jamie, "Sorry, we've only got the two."

Ed kicks off his shoes and starts putting on the overalls. Jamie looks over at Eric and notices his eyes are closed.

Sleep Eric.

Jamie comes closer, touches his hand. "Hey bro, you feeling alright?"

Eric opens his eyes, gives a small smile. "I'm trying to picture the pain as a ball of white light. Something sending a message I don't need to receive."

"Is it working?"

Eric smiles again, but it quickly morphs into an expression of agony. "I'm sorry," he says, as sweat forms around his mouth. "I'm sorry this is happening."

Jamie tries not to let the worry show on his face. "Man, the giant hole in the ocean wasn't your fault."

He expects his brother to smile at the stupid joke, but he doesn't. Instead, he looks like he wants to say something. His eyes keep flicking to Ed, to Matty.

"Be careful," he says. "Please."

"I will."

Ed and Matty finish pulling on the waders and gloves, and gather at the door. Jamie joins them, suddenly feeling exposed and vulnerable without thick rubber covering his legs. The captain taps his hook against the window with a *clink*.

"Matt, you grab the machete and we'll clear the freezer first. Then Jamie, you get in and grab that shovel as fast as you can. Scoop 'em up and throw 'em over, yeah?"

Jamie nods.

"Anything too big to scoop, Matty'll chop it," Ed says. "Move fast and watch for tails and teeth."

Eric does *not* look good, and Jamie has that sudden irrational fear again that something more is wrong than just a broken ankle. Something deeper. Matty groans again, shakes his head like maybe the stomachache is water in his ears that'll come flying out if he shakes hard enough.

Does Eric's skin look gray, or is that just the light?

He wants to go over and make sure Eric is still able to think clearly, to speak, to check his temperature, but Ed jabs him in the shoulder and says, "As soon as the door opens, we go. You ready?"

Jamie doesn't feel ready at all. He doesn't want to go outside, doesn't want to see the giant hole floating above his head. He doesn't want to see whatever has fallen on the deck. He wants to close his eyes and be back on dry land. He wants to get his brother to a hospital.

But he nods yes, and Ed says, "Okay. Let's go."

16

Ed turns the handle and struggles to push the door open. Too many fish are piled up against it. Jamie presses his shoulder to the door and shoves hard. The door inches across the deck, shoving creatures out of the way that snap with metallic-looking teeth as long and thick as framing nails.

As soon as there's enough space, Ed rushes outside with a roar, brandishing the gaff hook and swinging at anything that moves. Matty follows, sidestepping the tail of a creature that looks melted. Its body is covered in nasty looking spikes that stick out in all directions. It wiggles across the deck after Matty like its milky eyes can see him. Ed slams the hook down right through its head as Matty jumps over a thin body with a long snout and rows of layered teeth, not just in its mouth but surrounding its mouth. Ed hooks it through the middle and yells out as he struggles to lift the creature. The tail whips, a long dagger at the very end, and Ed narrowly avoids getting stabbed in the thigh as he throws the thing over the side.

Matty manages to grab the machete from the wall strap, and immediately begins slicing at every moving thing around him.

Ed clears a narrow path to the freezer hatch while Matty chops at a triangle-shaped creature whose skeleton looks like it's on the outside of its body. Ed hooks it off the hatch and Jamie ducks under his arm, throws it open, and jumps down into the dark.

An instant chill goes through him as his shoes crunch into the ice. There's just enough light shining to see the glint of the shovel blade. He grabs the handle and climbs back up the ladder, one handed, just as Matty swings the machete at a creature that looks to be all teeth. Layers of curved fangs spiral all the way down its open throat, and its misshapen body scurries across the deck toward Matty's leg. Behind him, more creatures gather, and that guttural, choking sound grows louder.

Ed screams from the other side of the freezer as three eel-like creatures whip their tails, covered in twisted barbs, at Ed's legs. Ragged lines tears open in the waiters and blood leaks out. Ed slams the hook down again and again, screaming the whole time.

Jamie runs up beside him and slams the shovel blade down on one eel's head, then another. He scoops up the bodies and throws them over the side. The snake-like creatures twist and unfurl as they fall into the dust scattered sky.

Matty, gripping the machete with both hands, slices through the skull of a fish with giant red eyes bulging out of its head. Its thick body keeps thrashing as dark blood spurts out of the gash. Matty's legs and chest are covered with silver scales, black blood, and chunks of meat.

Jamie places the flat shovel blade against the deck and runs forward, pushing the creatures toward the back of the boat, and starts throwing as many as he can overboard.

They've managed to clear half the deck, but in all the slashed bodies and severed pieces, it's hard to tell which ones are alive and which are dead. Jamie finds a rhythm, like digging a hole, of lifting a shovelful of parts and throwing it, then scooping again.

The blood-covered deck is slick and slimy with scales and guts, and Jamie struggles to keep his balance as he hoists each heavy creature over the side.

Jamie takes a break for a moment to wipe the salty sweat that rolls into his eyes and stings. One quick look at the deck, and Jamie thinks they've managed to kill or maim most of the deadly creatures. A few chopped up bodies still jerk sporadically, but most have been split in half, beheaded, or thrown into the sky. Even Ed stops to catch his breath, a wild-eyed look of victory on his face. He gives Jamie a quick smile and stabs a slow-moving creature with spines for fins right through the head.

He lets out a huff of air, says, "Aggressive bastards," and kneels next to the dead fish. He slips the gaff hook into the creature's mouth and twists until the jaws open, revealing rows of backward facing teeth, split at the ends like a devil's pitchfork.

Ed whistles, "Anything gets caught in there, it sure as hell ain't gettin' out."

Jamie takes a step back and hears a crunch under his shoe. He looks down to see teeth and spikes littering the deck, some so brittle they shatter like icicles. A few pieces are caught in the grooves between planks and stick straight up.

Jamie is about to tell Matty to watch out that he doesn't step on one, when he sees something move from the shadows at the aft. Something under a pile of destroyed creatures. The hill of scaled bodies shivers, scattering some of the pieces. One halved body spills its greasy guts out as it slides.

Jamie vaults over the freezer hatch, shovel in one hand, and elbows Matty out of the way just as a long, suckered tentacle shoots out from beneath the pile of fish and slaps onto the deck where he'd been standing. The tentacle lifts with a wet puckering sound and curls, hovering like a snake about to strike. The suction cups are ringed with bright blue, sharp fangs glistening at their centers. The deck is punctured with small round holes where each sucker fell.

Matty crouches down, a focused and intense look in his eyes, and swings the machete. It slices through the tentacle and sends the top half flying. He looks at Jamie and smiles, an expression that quickly vanishes as more tentacles emerge from the pile of fish bodies, one after the other, and Jamie realizes with some dreamlike kind of understanding, that there are more than eight arms earthworming toward them.

Ten, twenty, maybe even more, spread out to encircle the two men. The spikes in each sucker click on the deck like a woman's high heels. A moment later, the pile of fish collapses as something like an octopus with a transparent, bulbous head, as big as Jamie's torso, pulls itself out from under all the scales and guts and teeth. There's a flurry of motion and color underneath its translucent skin. A rhythmic pulsing that Jamie realizes are the animal's organs—its heart, brain, kidney, and stomach—each one glowing a different, bold color. The intestines, as green as fresh grass, are layered like a rolled-up hose. His brain struggles to make sense of all the arms attached to the rippling skin, color-changing to match the shadows, the silver fish scales, the wood pattern of the deck. Different patches of skin reflect different things.

The tentacles all seem to be the same length, and they all move as if each one has a mind of its own. As if each one is a hunter.

But it's the eyes that make tip Jamie off an edge he didn't even know he was standing on. Large, round, human-looking eyes. Black pupils with an explosion of color surrounding them. More human than human, it takes Jamie a second to register the eyes as being inside the head of an impossible creature.

The sight of it makes Jamie's scrotum tighten up, and he knows he either has to move or stay frozen. With a scream he rushes at the arms, holding the shovel blade down, and begins chopping each crawling tentacle. The skin is tougher than he expected, reminds him of stabbing thick foam wrapped in a tarp. It takes several stabs to cut through and separate a piece of one arm, that then writhes around on the deck, like maybe there's a brain in each tentacle.

Matty appears beside him, hacking away with the machete and screaming like a madman. Jamie cuts through one smaller tentacle that slithers toward Matty's foot, but another, larger one, rises and curls around the shovel handle. The spikes embed themselves in the wood and the whole tentacle flexes, snapping the shovel in half like a pencil.

The two pieces fall to the ground when Matty slashes through the base of the arm, then again through the severed appendage.

More arms keep appearing, crawling out of the shadows, and Jamie has the irrational thought that they'll never stop coming. That the creature can make them grow out of its body at will, unless...

Jamie kicks aside the still curling arm and grabs both pieces of his broken shovel—the blade and the handle, which now has a jagged fracture. As Matty swipes at one arm, then another, Jamie gets low and sneaks under a waving tentacle until he is eye to eye with the creature. He stares into that swirling galaxy at the center of the human-like eye and spears the shovel handle right into its center.

Something like a screech comes out of the animal and it backs away, all those tentacles thrashing. Jamie falls to the deck and rolls away, pieces of teeth dragging along his back, until he's out of range. The screeching reminds him of a hawk, a bird of prey.

Ed comes around to join Matty and Jamie as they watch the creature try and hide beneath all the fish carcasses. The arms seem have no purposeful motion now. The spiked suckers carve lines on the deck, scrape along the freezer with an ear-piercing shriek.

Jamie catches his breath while the creature's movement shudders to a halt. He looks around the deck of the ship and it's like a battlefield, strewn with blood and matter, slick with scales, putrid with stomach contents and guts. A battle, not against men, but against monsters none of them could have imagined existing. Monsters that fell from the sky.

A gentle rain begins to fall, and the coolness of it on his skin makes Jamie thankful. He uses the shovel blade to lift and throw heads, tails, and chunks of meat over the edge. He doesn't even watch them disappear into the darkness. Ed falls in next to him, hooking and throwing.

By the time they're finished, exhaustion creeps into Jamie's bones, and Ed's limping becomes more pronounced, as if his body finally allows itself to feel all the lacerations that cover his legs — wounds his adrenaline kept hidden from him until now.

The galley door opens and Eric stands there, flamingo-esque, his bad ankle hanging from one lifted leg. He supports himself by leaning against the jamb, one hand on either side, and looks out at the deck with a blank expression. His eyes meet his brother's and

Jamie wishes he could see all the words Eric won't say or doesn't know how to.

Once, when they were kids, Eric said his mind was like a train racing through the night with a long line of cars attached to it. He said those cars were covered in graffiti, and that paint spelled out all his thoughts, only the train was moving too fast to make sense of what they said.

Right now, Jamie wishes he could read the paint dripping on those cars.

His shoe scuffs against a fragment of tooth, sticking up from between the planks. He kneels and wiggles it back and forth to loosen it so no one else steps on it. Rain continues to fall with a soft sound, pattering on his neck, running down his back.

He looks up and sees Matty standing with his face turned toward the sky, the ocean, one hand holding his stomach again. His mouth is open to the rain, and he lets the drops fall on his tongue.

He looks over at Jamie briefly, tries to smile and it turns into a grimace. "I'm so thirsty," he says.

Jamie turns back to the piece of tooth, finally wrenches it free, and notices a small puddle of rainwater in a dent on the metal freezer hatch. It ripples with each new drop, creating rings within rings. An echo of an echo.

Moonlight glows around the boat, giving it a halo against the night sky they float through, and some of that light illuminates the puddle.

Something moves inside it.

A trick of the light?

Jamie tilts his head and leans in closer. Thin, white strings wriggle in the water, twisting and turning, as thin as sewing thread. A raindrop lands on the back of his hand, and within the tiny splash, he sees another thin worm. He shakes it off his hand and stands, looks up at the rain. With that halo glow from the moon, he watches the drops fall like they're in slow motion, and the light shines through the droplets, and within each one is a small, twisted thread.

He looks over at Matty, at his open mouth catching water, and yells, "Matty, stop! Don't drink that! Close your mouth!"

Matty looks at him in surprise, and Jamie realizes it doesn't matter because Matty already let the water fall on his tongue before. Back before they all went into the galley, he stood there just like he is now and let the rain fall into him. And that's when he got the stomachache.

Jamie yells, "Ed, get Matty inside!" Then turns to his brother, "Eric, get inside!"

Eric doesn't seem to hear him. He's gazing up at the ocean. Jamie turns to see what his brother is looking at, and that's when hundreds of strands of white filament come pouring down out of the hole. It makes Jamie think of tassels on a graduation cap, these brilliant threads fall in straight lines, still attached to something inside the dark hole, like climbing ropes lowered into a cave, and hang there like a shredded curtain. Hundreds of them land on the deck, stretching all the way back up into the darkness.

Something comes, not falling exactly, but floating downward. A human shape, suspended by dozens of white threads, silhouetted against the black circle above it.

17

Ed hobbles backward and lets out a cry of, "Holy shit," followed by, "What the fuck?"

Drops of rain keep drizzling into Matty's still open mouth.

At first, Jamie wonders if it's another fish, a bigger one, coming down out of the hole, but this is so clearly human that his skin goes cold. The person looks like a skydiver gently floating down to earth, all those white filaments like the strings of a balloon or a parachute.

Hopping on one foot, Eric comes outside, keeping a hand on the wheelhouse wall to stay balanced. He doesn't take his eyes off the figure coming down to them like something straight out of the Bible, and Jamie remembers hearing in church that the people in those stories were terrified when they saw an angel. Which is why the angels always said, "Do not be afraid."

But this thing has no wings. There's no choir. It says nothing. Just silently slides down the sky, arms outstretched, wrists hanging limply.

As it gets closer, Jamie's head feels like it's disconnecting from his body. He recognizes the light blue shirt, the beige shorts. He tells himself that it can't be, there's no way…

…until he sees the one white shoe. The other shoe, its mate, is either somewhere on the deck, or thrown off the side with all the creatures.

A.J.

His lifeless body descends, closer and closer to the deck, with dozens of white threads wrapped around his arms, legs, neck, head, and torso, making it appear as though he's been wrapped in the web of a giant spider. The threads slow until the tips of A.J.'s feet hover right above the carnage on the deck.

Jamie has just enough time to wonder about the intelligence of these white threads. Are they connected to a larger creature hidden within the hole? Are they some kind of animal reacting to its environment, and the trespassers it finds? Or is it operating with greater purpose?

These questions race through Jamie's mind only seconds before one of his questions is answered, as the threads wrapped around A.J.'s head pull tighter and lift his face, exposing his open throat. Coiled around the inside of his throat, like fishing line around a reel, are more white threads. They vibrate and go blurry, causing a raspy hum to emit from the esophagus.

A single note, like a band leader at the start of the song getting the rest of the band in tune.

More threads emerge from A.J.'s mouth, their ends curl around his lips and dig into the skin, leaving tiny bloodless holes. Jamie thinks of stitches, of a needle pulling string to close an open cut. These threads open the jaw and that humming sound becomes a breathy *Ehhhhhh.* A salt-soaked wind blowing the opening of a cave.

A.J.'s cloudy eyes stare straight ahead.

The threads twist again and the mouth closes, pressing the teeth together, making the hum sound like *Rrrrrrr,* before tightening the lips and turning it into a *Iiiiiiii.* Then finally, the threads embedded in A.J.'s cheeks coil, pulling his lips back and the hum changes one last time into a hard K sound before trailing off into a breathy hiss.

A.J.'s head turns and the eyes point at Matty. He grips his stomach tighter and backs away, hyperventilating. The white threads turn the head once more to Ed, then Jamie, before coming to rest on Eric.

In a series of coordinated movements, the threads operate in unison as the hum continues, putting together all the sounds it created.

Ehhhhhh

Rrrrrrrrr

Iiiiiiiiiiii

Kkkkkkk

Eric recognizes his name only seconds before Jamie does. His hand against the wall slips and he staggers forward, struggling to remain upright, and his mouth falls open, his face an expression of fearful surprise. Jamie thinks he's never seen his brother look more vulnerable or afraid.

Ehhh Rrrrr Iiiii Kkkkk

Threads crawl along A.J.'s right arm, twisting around the skin from shoulder to hand, stretching along the length of the fingers. The arm lifts until it's straight, and that hand is open, palm up, pointed at Eric in a gesture of invitation.

Marionette.

That's the word Jamie was searching for. The threads, these so-white-they're-almost-silver filaments are like the strings of a puppeteer, and an invisible hand inside that dark hole pulls on them to animate the corpse at their ends.

Eric falls back against the wheelhouse. His good leg folds and he slides down until he sits on the deck, his broken ankle straight out in front of him.

Ed is frozen, watching the dead man with the open throat speak, move, beckon. Matty is doubled over in pain, still holding the machete and keeping the pointed end dug into the deck, leaning on it like a crutch.

There are four people on the deck, but this corpse only wants one of them. The man who killed him.

Jamie moves to run to his brother, shove him inside the galley, drag him if he has to, when he feels something slithering past his feet. He looks down and sees dozens of strands of filament crawling along the deck around him. Stretching past him like the roots of a tree growing in fast forward, headed straight for Eric.

Eric backs away on his hands, pushing with his one good foot, toward the galley door, but the threads are too fast. The white threads move with singular purpose, slithering in broken lines. They slide under Eric's deformed ankle and wrap around it like a python around its prey.

Eric screams in pain as the threads go taut, pull him back. Jamie rushes to his brother and stomps on the filaments as hard as he can. They feel hard and rubbery on his feet. Thin but solid. They don't even loosen, no matter how hard he stomps.

He kneels and tries to pry them off Eric's leg as his brother is dragged over the deck, closer to A.J.'s hovering body.

Ehhhhhh

Rrrrrrrr

Iiiiiiiiiiii

Kkkkkkkk

Eric screams again and Jamie hears something snap. A white fragment of jagged bone comes ripping out of Eric's shin as the filament tightens. Eric screams as the shape of his leg changes and all the skin on his face goes as pale as a full moon. His scream turns into something more like wailing, and the back of his head bounces off the deck as the threads drag him closer.

Jamie looks to Ed, then to Matty. "Help me!" he yells.

Ed finally snaps out of his trance, shakes his head once, and runs over. Matty stands up straight, teeth clenched, one arm holding his stomach, and

Jamie can't tell if it's sweat or rain that runs down his face.

Jamie grabs both of Eric's forearms and pulls, feeling the tension, the strength of the filaments as they fight against him. He looks up and A.J.'s dead eyes are staring right at him, and for one skipped heartbeat Jamie thinks something is looking through the cloudy orbs. Watching him. Assessing him.

The filaments wrap tighter around Eric's leg, causing fresh blood to spurt from the hole where his bone sticks out. Other filaments move around on the deck, and Jamie thinks of a garden hose lying in the grass, water on, swaying back and forth like it's alive. He looks around for help and sees Ed in a crouch, slowly inching toward them.

Jamie has no choice but to let go. The harder he pulls, the harder those white tentacles pull back. Eric's shoes are now almost touching A.J.'s hovering feet, and the filaments raise the other arm, palm up. No longer beckoning, but welcoming.

Ehhhhhh

Rrrrrrrrr

Iiiiiiiiiiii

Kkkkkkkk

The voice, if that's what it is, sounds waterlogged. Like the lungs are full of fluid and syllables are being filtered through it, escaping in a raspy gurgle.

Ed sneaks behind A.J. and slams the gaff hook into his back. The animated corpse swings a little from his marionette strings, but he shows nothing. No pain, no aggression, not even anger. Ed growls and stabs A.J. again, this time in the chest. White filament instantly shoots out of the hole and coils itself around A.J.'s shoulder and arm.

Eric howls as he's pulled closer, and the lower half of his ruined leg comes undone, as if the broken bone has completely separated from the rest of the leg and is now only attached by muscle and ligaments and skin.

It's that sound—his brother's howl of pain—that causes a panic in Jamie. Even more than Eric's pain, it's the tug of war with this dead thing, pulling his brother away from him that makes Jamie's heart beat frantically.

Without thinking, he rushes at A.J. and leaps into the air, wrapping his arms around the corpse's back. The threads that stretch up into the sky, all the way into the dark hole, go taut in response. A wave of rot fills Jamie's nostrils. Seawater and dead fish and salt and seaweed and putrid things feeding on decomposing flesh.

A.J.'s head doesn't turn so much as twist and hang down a little further so the chin touches Jamie's face. The cloudy eyes look at him and Jamie hears the gargled breathing, feels it bubbling inside the chest. He feels the tentacles slide against him as they tighten.

Something in the eyes moves. More white threads, wrapping themselves around the faded black pupils, and Jamie wonders if all these threads (pieces of something larger and intelligent) can see him through those eyes.

"Matty!" Jamie yells. "Cut them! Cut them down!"

Matty snaps upright when he hears Jamie's voice. He looks down at the machete like he forgot he's holding it. He lifts it in both hands like it's a sword, and runs forward, teeth bared in pain.

The threads pull and drag Eric further across the deck, lifting A.J. and Jamie up into the air. Eric screams even louder and his leg seems to elongate. His feet are in the air, now, and his shoulders are scraping through the scales and blood. Any more tension and Jamie knows it's going to rip right off, and there's no fighting the pull of the threads. They'll yank A.J. (with Jamie clinging to him) right up into the hole like they're fish on a line, and Eric's leg will tear at the knee, dropping him back down to the boat to bleed out until the threads wrap around him again, (like a spider spinning web around prey) and to yank him back up.

"Matty, cut them!" Jamie yells again.

And Matty comes running. Mouth open now, making the gauze on his face go bright with fresh blood. He jumps as high as he can and slices the machete through half the threads above A.J.'s head.

It's enough.

Jamie feels the right side of A.J.'s body go limp, as those threads that kept him animated go twirling into the ocean night. His body lowers, feet to the deck. Matty lands with a wince, and immediately slashes at the threads attached to Eric's leg. They thrash wildly, a powerline on the ground after a storm. Matty grabs Eric's armpits and pulls him away, and the second he's free, Jamie plants his feet on the deck and pushes forward with all his strength. To his surprise, A.J. goes with him.

He tackles the corpse into the railing, trying to shove him overboard for the second time tonight. A.J.'s spine hits the metal rod and Jamie hears a crack from deep inside the moving body. The upper half folds over the edge backward. More cracks and snaps that would make Jamie sick if he wasn't struggling against something not alive.

The threads controlling A.J.'s left side move his leg and hook it around Jamie's. The left arm comes up and thuds across his back, the wrist locking against his ribs at a ninety-degree angle.

A.J. is slipping over the railing and Jamie can't untangle himself. His feet leave the deck as A.J.'s body tumbles backward, taking Jamie with it.

The last thing Jamie sees, before he's looking down into the white dust of the galaxy scattered across black canvas, is Matty's haggard face and the gleam of a blade hacking away. A.J.'s arm releases its grip and Jamie shoves the body away then starts grasping for something, anything to hold onto.

A.J.'s body drifts away, broken, contorted, slowly turning against the night sky, and disappears.

For one heartbeat, Jamie's neurons fire in a burst of light and memory. Flooding his mind with images of past, present, and future. He sees everything all at once. Every memory a photograph, every physical sensation. Every sight, taste, and smell flood his brain. He'll fall until the oxygen thins and he can no longer breathe. He'll fall until he can't feel the fall. He'll face that cosmic dust and soar into it like Icarus going backwards.

He's ready.

He's not ready.

He hears an infant's cry and it tugs at him. A voice so new and raw it sounds terrified. He wants to comfort it. His son.

His arms still flail, hands and fingers outstretched, and he feels cold metal touch his palm. His fingers close immediately and the fall ends.

Jamie hangs from the railing, chest banging against the hull of the boat.

He looks up and sees Matty leaning over the edge, reaching out a hand. Jamie glances down at his feet dangling above space. Endless everything surrounds him, and he remembers why he knows the constellations that dot the blackness beneath him. It's a pattern. Tiny dots that form images, and he remembers Sleep Eric sitting at the kitchen table making the same pattern with pencil and paper.

Matty grabs his arm and pulls.

18

Just when Jamie thinks he can't hold on any longer, Ed appears at the railing and grabs his other arm. Together, the two men drag Jamie up the side of the boat and back onto the deck.

Jamie wants to crawl over to Eric and check on him, but he has no strength. He collapses on the deck, looking up into the dark hole, the white filaments fluttering as they are drawn back into the void.

That black circle looms over them like the eye of a predator. Holding them in place. Watching.

Jamie rolls over to his stomach and army-crawls through the slime and blood until he comes to Eric's side. His breathing is labored and shallow, and Jamie feels completely helpless. He wishes he knew what to do. He thinks *tourniquet* but isn't sure if this is the right situation or not. Sometimes a wound needs blood flow, and he doesn't know the difference.

He strokes Eric's face like he would his own child and whispers to him.

"Hang on. Just hang on as long as you can. I know it hurts but I need you to stay focused and keep breathing."

Jamie looks around at all the scales and spikes and jagged pieces of teeth scattered on the deck. He worries about infection, but more than that, he fears the next creature, the next thing that comes looking for his brother. Because one thing is certain, and that's whatever is inside the dark hole, wants Eric. More than the others, it wants him. Even the first fish they found, the one inside the galley, all those white worms came after him. Ed was closer, but they reached for Eric.

"Eric, listen, we need to move you, okay? I'm going to help you sit up and then get you inside."

Eric groans in response. Then, "Is my leg still there?"

"Yeah. It's in bad shape, but it's still there."

"I don't think I can move," Eric wheezes.

Jamie helps him sit up, tries not to look at the damaged leg, at the way it lies mangled and bent. He crouches down in front of his brother, with his back to him, and says, "Put your hands on my shoulders."

Eric does what he's asked.

"I'm going to stand," Jamie says. "Just push up with your other leg as much as you can."

Holding onto Eric's wrists, Jamie stands, pulling his brother's weight with him. Eric yells out as his bad leg rises.

They shuffle toward the galley door. Eric's hands and arms are cold and sweaty. They're about to go inside when Matty screams from behind them. Jamie turns and sees Matty fall to his knees, both arms held to his stomach, face creased in agony. Blood dribbles from between his lips.

Ed lowers himself next to his son and places a hand on his back. "Is there any pain in your chest? Your lungs?"

Matty breathes hard and fast. He tries to speak and spits blood on his dad's shirt. He doubles over, face turning bright red.

"Matthew," Ed says, and there's so much fear in his eyes that Jamie feels for him. His son is in extraordinary pain and there's nothing he can do. Less than nothing.

Matty screams again and Ed turns his gaze to Eric.

"Did you do this?" He points at his son and yells, "Did you do this?"

Jamie shifts Eric's weight and helps him stand on his one good leg, keeping an arm around his shoulder.

"Ed, no," Eric says weakly. "No."

Ed stands, leaving Matty folded up and holding his stomach, rocking back and forth.

"Tell me the truth, Fletcher. Did you give him something? Some powder in a little baggie?" He says this last part with a mocking tone, and that's when Jamie realizes he's still holding the gaff hook in his right hand. Without the handle, it almost looks like a prop from a pirate movie.

Ed takes a couple steps closer, growing unnervingly calm, the hook swinging gently from his hand. "Why does this," pointing the hook up at the hole in the ocean, "want you so bad?"

Behind Ed, Matty struggles to his feet and moans, "Dad. Stop."

Jamie glances at the puddle of rainwater on top of the freezer hatch. Several of the tiny worms swim into a cluster, tying themselves into a long, twisted knot. It crawls out of the water and slides along the metal, head bobbing like it's sniffing for food.

Matty tries to walk and yells out in pain again.

Ed lowers the hook to his side. "Is this fentanyl? Did you slip him the same stuff you gave the other kid?"

"Ed, I swear to you I didn't give him anything," Eric says.

The captain shakes his head slowly. "I don't believe you," and cocks the hook back like it's a tennis racket. A voice screams "Dad, no!" and a blur moves between the two men just as Ed flicks the hook forward. Matty grunts as a ragged, gaping line opens across his belly.

The hook clatters to the ground, coated in blood, and Ed's eyes widen in horror. Matty falls to his knees, blood pouring from his stomach.

Ed kneels in front of him. "No, no, no, no, no!" He presses a hand to the wound, but bright red fluid keeps gushing around Ed's fingers.

"Oh Matt, I'm so sorry. I'm so sorry."

Matty's body sways and his eyes roll from side to side, unfocused, then he slumps over on his back. Jamie helps his brother back down and kneels beside Ed.

"We can try and sew it up. Maybe slow the bleeding," Jamie says.

Ed moves his hand away, his face a mask of complete shock, and Jamie lifts up Matty's shirt. As soon as he sees the opening, he knows there's no stitching it back together. The intestines are exposed, but they look different than Jamie expects. Hard, almost armor-looking segments, covered in slick blood. He's seen his share of cows and pigs slaughtered, and he once helped field dress an elk on a hunting trip. What's inside Matty doesn't look like guts at all.

The armor plating moves, slides across the inside of Matty's belly, and Jamie scrambles backward as a narrow head emerges. A large white eye with a tiny black dot at the center. It uncoils like a snake as it slithers out of the gash in Matty's stomach, the head swinging slowly back and forth. It hits the deck with a thud, its mouth opening to reveal rows of uneven, glasslike teeth. The back is coated in segments of gray armor plating that pulse a bluish-purple color.

Matty jerks like he's having a seizure as the creature drags its long body out of his stomach. Ed yells, "Matt, no! Look at me, son. Look at me!"

An eel, Jamie thinks. *A cross between an eel and a centipede.*

The creature's tail slides out, leaving a gaping bloody wound, and Matty's body goes still. Ed lifts his son's head and cradles it, tears falling from his eyes. The creature is as long as Matty, its belly scratching along the deck as its snout weaves closer to Eric. Jamie's instinct is to grab the tail but he doesn't want the head to whip around and take a chunk out of him. And he can't be sure there isn't something just as sharp as the teeth on the underside.

Eric does his best to push back toward the galley, but the eel-creature's white-circle eyes land on him and the thing slithers forward, its body curving like three Ss hooked together. Jamie looks around for something to grab and use to hit the thing, when Ed's legs go marching past. The captain walks right up to the creature, raises his right foot, and stomps on the creature's head. The eel-creature's body stiffens straight, then spasms.

If any of those teeth cut through Ed's shoe and pierced his foot, he shows no signs of pain. Dark liquid, shiny bits of teeth, and goo are visible when Ed lifts his foot and brings it down again even harder. Matter sprays out, and Jamie feels bits of it splatter on his face.

The captain turns to Eric, almost to the galley, now, and stares at him, chest heaving. His flannel shirt is torn and soaked with his son's blood. If Ed attacks, Jamie knows he won't be able to stop him. He can try, but the man is too big and powerful, and with the amount of anger rushing through him, Jamie won't stand a chance.

Eric and Ed stare at one another, each of them frozen in place.

Finally, Eric says, "Ed, I'm so sorry."

The captain's face seems to age in seconds as creases appear around his eyes and mouth. Tears run down the lines into his beard. He nods slowly and steps away from the creature he just destroyed. He goes back to his son, sniffling, and slips his arms underneath the body. With a groan, Ed lifts Matty off the deck. His head lolls back and the lifeless, open eyes gaze uselessly at Jamie. The cords in Ed's neck strain with the weight as he walks to the edge of the deck and looks out at an upside-down horizon.

One of Matty's eyes shifts a little and the pupil rolls to the side. Jamie squints and takes a step closer to his brother. The hairs on his arms rise. Small, black antennae come poking out from around the eyeball, moving erratically, followed by jagged pincers and a coarse body with spindly legs. The body skitters over the bridge of Matty's nose, the rest of it still inside his eye socket. Another comes out of the nose and crawls along the cheek while another exits the partially open mouth. Creatures as long as Jamie's hand scurry across the face and up Ed's arm. He has to feel it, but he doesn't acknowledge the sensation. Instead, he stands at the railing and Jamie hears him whispering something. He takes a step closer to hear, then Ed falls forward without a sound.

His waist hits the railing and his upper body disappears over the side, followed by his legs, shooting up as if caught and yanked by an invisible snare, and he's gone.

Jamie runs to the railing and leans over, sees Ed soaring into the infinite darkness, his son still clutched in his arms.

LOW TIDE

19

Jamie watches until the two bodies are lost to space, to the stars. He becomes aware of how quiet the boat is without water pressing on all sides. Without waves rolling against the hull.

He hears something hit the deck and turns to see Eric dragging himself to the wheelhouse, where he sits against the wall and leans his head back, breathing fast and hard. Jamie comes over and sits next to him, shoulder to shoulder, and they both look up at the ocean in the sky. The waves roll at one speed in the distance and slow the closer they get to the dark hole.

A perfect circle, Jamie thinks.

The hole is rimmed with white, agitated water that flows inward and disappears. It looks so much like a hollow eye—an eye without depth or emotion, without pupil or iris—that Jamie hates the way it hovers above them, watching without blinking.

What can you do against something like that?

Jamie looks at his brother's leg and tries not to think about the damage beneath the surface. Fragments of bone floating in blood. Severed nerves and torn cartilage. It makes his stomach hurt to look at it. Makes his own legs weak.

Glassy beads of sweat form and trace salty lines down Eric's face. His eyes squeeze together as he shifts position. Jamie hears the grind of his teeth.

It's quiet. The hole above them produces no sound that Jamie is aware of. And if it does, he's so used to it now that it's background static. Even the ocean, that stretches from one end of his vision to the other, doesn't sound like the ocean, and he has the sense, again, that they are contained within something. Something that blocks out the world.

"After all this time," Eric says weakly, "after not seeing you for so long, I honestly hoped this trip would help you somehow. Help you make sense of things."

Jamie thinks, but doesn't say, *If I have to go, at least it's not alone. At least it's with you.*

"Tell me about him," Eric says.

Jamie looks over and his brother's eyes are still closed.

"Who?"

"The kid," Eric says. "Tell me all about my nephew."

"Dylan," Jamie, gazing back up at the hole.

"I like the name," Eric smiles.

Jamie takes a deep breath and says, "Something doctors don't tell you is how weak a baby is. When we first brought him home, I was nervous to hold him. They can't hold their head up very well, you know? It wobbles all over the place. And they don't smile right away. That takes time. So, it feels like a fragile doll."

Eric shifts again and a small sound escapes him.

"He's got reddish hair. Sylvie calls it 'strawberry blond' and maybe she's right. All her friends say he's a ginger, but I think it's lighter than that. He sits up on his own now and smiles a lot. You can see his personality starting to come through. Some kids are really serious, but I can already tell Dylan is going to be joyful. He smiles at just about everything."

Eric, with his eyes closed, smiles too, and Jamie notices a small red bump on his brother's neck. Just under the hairline. It's almost a geometric shape, and Jamie thinks back to Sleep Eric, to the way he'd rub his neck after a night of sleepwalking. He wonders if that strange bump has always been there.

"He laughs easily, too, and makes sounds," Jamie says. "Not words, you know, but these cute noises. We have one of those baby monitors in his room and sometimes, early in the morning, Sylvie and I will listen and watch him. We call it the 'Dylan Show,' and we'll have coffee and watch him."

Jamie pats the phone in his pocket on instinct. "I'd show you a picture but…"

Eric shakes his head, "No, this is better." His breathing has slowed down a little. "When you first found out that she was pregnant, were you scared?"

Jamie laughs. "Hell yeah, man. Terrified. It was the unknown."

"Did you hope the kid would be a boy or a girl?"

The question surprises Jamie. It seems so unlike something his brother would ask, and it begins to scratch the surface of why he was so afraid in the first place. He sees that now. It's so simple and obvious, and the only reason he didn't see it before was because he didn't want to dig down to where the answers lay buried.

His fear, it wasn't Sylvie, or commitment, and it wasn't even the baby.

It was him.

Always him.

"I wanted it to be a girl," Jamie says.

"Why?"

Of course, he'd ask.

"Why?" Jamie repeats.

He sighs and does his best to not feel fear as he gazes into the dark, silent hole.

"Shit, man. Because I didn't want a boy. When you're a dad to a girl, you just have to love and respect her. Show her how the men in her life should treat her. At least that's what I thought. But with a boy, you have to raise him to be a man."

He pictures Dylan's face, his toothless smile. If he concentrates, he can almost hear the boy's laugh, can feel what it does to his heart when he sees his son smile. The smoothness of his skin, the softness of his hair, the heat of him when he lies on Jamie's chest.

"I was afraid," Jamie says, "because I didn't think I knew how to raise a boy. Maybe no one does.

But I was scared of what might be *in* him, you know? The shit that's in us."

Eric smiles, eyes still closed. "Might be in me more than you."

Jamie shakes his head. Tears burn his eyes. "That's why I'm here."

Eric's eyes open, turn to his brother.

"It came out of nowhere...the anger," Jamie says. He holds his thumb and forefinger a few centimeters apart. "I was this close to hitting her. She said some shit and I took it bad. Something flared up in me so fast I didn't even have time to think about what it was, or why it was there. My arm came up, and my hand was a fist. Dylan, man, he's sitting there on the floor listening to us scream at each other and his eyes look like he has no idea what's about to happen. But Sylvie does, and she just stands there, waiting for me to do it. I felt like I had a match in my hand, and I'd covered them both with gasoline, and her eyes seemed to be asking me, 'Are you going to burn it all down?'"

"But you didn't do it," Eric says.

"I didn't do it."

"How many times did we see Dad beat up Mom?"

Jamie shakes his head, blinks hard and wipes his eyes. *Too many*, he thinks. And what does that do to a kid? It was like a bony hand with strips of rotted flesh reaching into his brain, grabbing wires, important ones, ones that matter, and plugging them into all the wrong places. Everyone says what you're not supposed to do, but no one ever tells you how not to do it. Especially when it's the only thing you know. The only example you've ever seen.

"And every time," Eric continues, "we felt like we were the ones getting hit instead."

Jamie remembers that, too. A physical pain that didn't belong to him. But sometimes Dad took his anger out on the boys, too. More on Eric than Jamie. Was that because he was older?

"You were gonna get tested at some point," Eric says. "I did, and I failed. You passed."

He smiles, "I'm proud of you."

Jamie can't stop the tears, now. All that guilt, the shame, over something he didn't actually do. He still felt the weight of *wanting* to do it, but maybe that wasn't the crime. The crime was what he did next.

He ran.

He came to Hawaii to be with the one person he thought could understand and found that person farther gone than he expected. But, maybe not. Maybe that's why Eric never married or had kids. The match still burned and needed somewhere to go. He still hurt people, but they weren't people he loved.

And now we're here…

Something stirs in the darkness above them. Something twisting inside that hole.

Jamie stands and shields his eyes from the moonlight shining underneath the boat. He sees flashes of color, ribbons of it curving around the inside of the hole like it's a tunnel.

"Do you see that?" Jamie asks.

The ribbons of the color twist, becoming clearer as they get closer to the edge of the hole, and then they slip out, lowering into the sky. Jamie counts at least twelve of them, thicker than the white filaments that brought A.J. down, these glow blue with a bright pink ridge of light that ripples along the edges.

Eric stares up at the hole, watching as the ribbons descend, a look of resignation on his face.

"They won't stop," Eric says.

Jamie looks around for the dropped weapons. "I'll take the machete, and you take the hook," then stops.

"What do you mean, 'they'?"

20

"Ed was right," Eric says as he lowers his chest to the deck. "They want me. I've known for a long time they'd want me back. It's no accident we came out here tonight, to this spot. And it's no accident they were waiting."

Jamie spots the machete and picks it up. The ribbons dangle from the hole, fluttering like something alive.

Eric says, "When they have me, I think they'll stop. I think they'll leave you alone."

"You keep saying 'they' and I don't know what that means."

"They're making something new. They want to start over and they know the process is destructive, but there's no other way."

Jamie gets on his knees next to Eric, looks him in the eye. "Who the fuck are they?"

Eric doesn't say anything, just looks at his brother, and memories start flooding Jamie's mind. Waking up in the middle of the night as Eric climbed out of bed. Following him downstairs, through the house, and outside into the cold air. Watching him walk across the street to stand under the broken streetlamp, like he was waiting for something. His young boy-body, a dark silhouette in a solid beam of light that shone down on him as the streetlamp came on.

But it wasn't the streetlamp, was it? It came from higher up than that. A spotlight shining down from the sky.

You didn't know what it was, so you accepted the easiest answer.

And when that light shut off, Eric was gone. Gone for hours.

Sleep Eric.

How tired he was the next day. Tired and worn out. Eyes, bloodshot. Skin cold. No memory of where he'd been or what he saw.

Mom saying, "Your brother sleepwalks. Keep an eye on him. Make sure he doesn't hurt himself."

Eric, climbing up into the tree and looking up at the stars. Waiting. Always waiting for the next time.

Awake Eric changed, and all this time Jamie thought it was because of Dad, and maybe it still was. But Eric lived each day wondering when they'd come for him again. When they'd call him, steal him away from all the stress of their home, the hurt of Dad staying, and another kind of hurt when he left.

Jamie shakes his head, and his eyes are burning again. "You should have told me."

Eric tries to smile, and it turns into a grimace of pain.

"How do you explain something like that?" he says. "I don't really understand it, but I know things.

Like, in a place somewhere in me where there aren't words."

He flattens both hands on the deck. "Take care of yourself, bro. Go back home. Tell her you were wrong." He smiles. "You're going to be exactly the dad that kid needs."

Eric begins pulling himself forward, his damaged leg dragging behind him. Rain falls again, making sounds as the drops hit the wheelhouse, the freezer, the deck. Jamie looks up, tastes salt as a few drops land in his mouth, and sees the ribbons come even closer. Each one is as wide as his chest, and he can hear the thick, rubbery flapping as they twist lower and lower.

Jamie knows they are alive, connected to something else much larger. Something in the hole that has been seeking Eric for as long as he's been running. Jamie knows this the same way Eric said he *knew* things. In a place so deep there aren't words.

"Eric, come on man, let's figure this out together," Jamie says. His fingers tighten around the machete's handle. He braces himself to run forward and slash at those ribbons the moment they touch the deck.

Eric ignores him and keeps crawling, dragging his body through the debris of so many creatures until he reaches the center of the deck. He rolls onto his back and stares directly up into the sky, at the ribbons coming straight toward him.

"Don't do this, Eric!" Jamie shouts. "Please! Stay here."

Eric smiles at his brother as the blue and pink ribbons coil on the deck and begin moving. They slip under Eric's arms and wrap around his chest, curl around his waist and legs.

He grips the machete tighter, preparing to hack away, but he can't move.

"Don't go!" he yells. "Please, Eric. Don't let them take you!"

Within seconds, Eric's body is mostly covered by the flowing ribbons, and without a sound they begin to draw back up toward the hole, lifting Eric into the air. He hovers there for a moment, suspended by these bright, colorful ribbons.

"Eric, please don't go!"

But he's already in the sky.

There's something gentle to the way the ribbons pull Eric up, as if they're cradling him. Something fragile they are afraid to break. Jamie watches, rain falling into his eyes and stinging, along with his tears. A feeling comes over him, one he hasn't felt in the same way, and so strongly, since the night Eric disappeared from under that streetlamp.

Loneliness.

Abandonment.

An ache in his heart so powerful he thought it might stop beating.

Halfway up, the ribbons slow and stop moving, leaving Eric suspended in their coils. Light begins to emanate from within all those folds. A warm orange light that grows in intensity.

Jamie hears Eric's voice echoing down from the sky. It starts as a yell and grows in depth until it becomes a full-throated scream of agony.

"Eric! No, no, no, no, no, no!"

The light is now so bright it hurts to look at. It encompasses Eric's entire body, seems to come only from him, from inside him, and not the ribbons.

The scream turns to distortion, the sound of something ripped apart, then there's a muffled explosion and Eric's body completely disintegrates. The shape of him turns into millions of fuzzy points of light, each one with substance. They flow from within the ribbons, surrounding them, and fall upward, forming a teardrop as they move toward the dark hole only to scatter across the ocean and glow on the water.

All at once, the ribbons uncoil and hang limp once more, before whatever they are attached to resumes pulling them, leaving the shining dust of Eric hanging in the atmosphere. Soon, the ribbons have vanished back into the hole and the glowing particles continue to fall up. Some of the dust drifts down, like flakes of ash, toward the boat, and Jamie stares as they float like dandelion blossoms. A piece here, a piece there. They alight on the deck, the railing, and spread out like a bright orange moss. Patches appear all over the boat.

As he watches all these pieces fall, the dark hole turns a lighter shade of black, then another, and another. It becomes dark gray, then light gray, then a silver that reflects the moonlight. The hole no longer has depth. There's something right there, just out of view.

Jamie sucks in a breath and holds it as something, the size and shape of the dark hole, slips out from inside it. A perfect circle, bright and metallic that shimmers with the distorted ripples of everything beneath it reflected on its surface. It slides across the sky, twisting as it does, becomes vertical to the left of the ship. A giant silver circle that continues to slide until it's underneath the boat. Jamie looks up briefly and the hole is gone. The ocean has rushed back into place and is now one solid body of water.

Jamie runs to the railing and leans over. The silver disc hovers below him, filling his field of vision. The polished surface is unlike anything he's ever seen. Strange symbols that hurt his head to stare at are etched along the edge and continue all the way around. It's hard to tell if it's spinning or not because of the way it mirrors the ocean, the sky, the boat, but Jamie feels a sense of motion from the object, all the blood in him vibrating with whatever propulsion system gives this thing flight.

The vibrations grow more intense until Jamie fears his blood is going to come streaming out of his skin, drop by drop, followed by a deep hum that reverberates in his bones. They feel suddenly heavier, like they're made of stone, and he sinks to the deck. His hand plunges into a patch of orange moss. His fingers sink into the silky soft fibers as his lungs struggle to get air. He lies back on the deck and closes his eyes, feeling like his entire skeleton is being magnetically pulled toward the object, like it's going to rip out of his body, break through the deck, the hull, and shoot straight onto the metallic surface beneath him.

He's paralyzed as the hum grows even louder. But it's not something he hears. He feels it, in every part of himself. He's pressed against the deck, searching for signals that control his voice. He finds them, slowly, and begins to scream.

The boat twists in the air, spinning in place, and Jamie's view changes from ocean, to horizon, to sky, to the metallic circle.

There is a deep blare of sound that shakes Jamie's skull, and the disc-shaped object grows smaller, but he can't tell if it's because the object is rising into the sky, or if he's falling away from it.

Pressure crushes his chest and his breath comes in shallow gasps as he tries to scream again, but no sound escapes.

His ears are overwhelmed with the roar of blood rushing through his head. He doesn't understand how his ribs haven't collapsed yet.

The disc gets smaller and smaller, and soon it disappears against the blue of an early morning sky. The pressure is gone, and Jamie feels the gentle lapping of waves against the boat.

He closes his eyes and slips into a deep and dreamless sleep.

21

Jamie opens his eyes to see white clouds drifting across a light blue sky. He sits up and puts a hand to his head, sees orange and pinkish hues bleeding up from the horizon. Seagulls squawk and float lazily above him. A cool breeze caresses his face.

He gets to his feet and stumbles around the wheelhouse to the front of the boat. Before him is sand, and beyond that, palm trees. Nothing but miles of beach in either direction. He sees the roofs of houses that lie up in the hills and wonders if they can see him, if any of them have called the police, or the Coast Guard.

The boat has run aground, tilted on the shore.

Jamie has this strange, dreamlike feeling as he searches through his memories of the last several hours. He remembers everything, but the events seem filtered through a consciousness that isn't his own. He looks around the deck at all the scales, the slime, the bright blood, the smashed corpse of an unknown creature, and finally the orange patches of moss.

He remembers one of the last things Eric said to him.

They're trying to make something new.

He can't let that moss make it to shore, and he's not sure how he knows that. But he does.

Jamie wanders into the wheelhouse, over to the hatch he saw Matty go down earlier, and lifts it, then climbs the ladder down to the engine room. He finds a red, metal can with the word "fuel" scrawled on the side in permanent marker, then goes back up the ladder with the container in one hand.

Halfway up, he almost drops the fuel can when a spasm grips his stomach and twists until he thinks he's either going to vomit or faint. He waits for the wave of pain to pass, then climbs the rest of the way.

In the galley, Jamie opens drawers until he finds an old, rusty cigarette lighter and shoves it in his pocket, then goes outside.

The sound of the ocean hissing along the shoreline makes Jamie realize how thirsty he is. There will be plenty of time after he finishes his task.

He sets down the can, unscrews the cap, and turns his head away from the pungent fumes that escape. Then he picks it up and splashes the liquid all over the deck, making sure to soak each and every patch of surface. He pours a generous amount down the hatch that leads to the engine room and makes a trail on the floor from the wheelhouse, through the galley, and out to the deck. He pours until there's almost nothing left in the can.

The deck now shimmers in rainbow colors as sunlight glares off the liquid fuel. Patting his pocket to make sure he still has the lighter, Jamie goes to the front of the boat, splashes a little more fuel around, then climbs over the railing, and jumps down into the wet sand.

The boat looks so much bigger as he stands beside it. Bigger than it did the first time he saw it floating in the harbor. He tilts his head to read the words *Full Speed Ed* and it takes him a moment to remember that was also the name of a person.

Another spasm in his stomach makes him drop the can and clutch his belly with both arms. God, he wants to puke so bad. And the thirst is even stronger now. His mouth is as dry as the sand and it hurts to swallow.

He picks the can back up and splashes fuel onto the hull, then takes out the lighter and flicks it to a flame. He reaches out and touches it to the fuel. It catches immediately and trails up the side of the boat like a snake made of fire.

Jamie backs away and watches as the flames spread and grow, until the entire top deck of the ship is engulfed.

It's only a matter of time before the fire reaches the engine room, and Jamie doesn't want to be too close when that happens, so he starts walking down the beach. Toward what, he doesn't know.

When he gets about a hundred yards away, there is a massive explosion and a blast of heat hits his back. He turns around and sees a fireball billowing smoke into the sky. Pieces of debris soar in arcs with black trails.

Jamie wraps his arms tighter around his stomach as another wave of pain grips him. It feels like something is ripping at his insides. He sits down in the sand and watches the *Full Speed Ed* consumed by flames and presses a hand to his belly. He feels something hard just under the surface, something that squirms and moves away from his touch, causing another burst of pain that makes sweat break out on his back and face.

His vision spins so he closes his eyes, but even the light keeps spinning, and he sees faces in that light.

Eric.

Sylvia.

Dylan.

It hurts - how much he wants to see Eric one more time. It hurts - how much he wants to lie in Sylvie's arms and watch their son on the monitor, hear his coos and babbling words. He wants to press his face to that little boy's head and breathe him in. He wants to tell them both how sorry he is, even though Dylan won't understand it, he still wants to say the words. Maybe the first word Dylan will ever say is "sorry" and would that be such a bad thing?

His thoughts are overwhelmed with a singular desire for water. Jamie has never been this thirsty in his life, has never felt the burning need for water as much as he does now.

He gets on his hands and knees and crawls toward the ocean. The sensation when the water hits his legs is almost too much for him. He kneels in the waves, lets them wash over him, and feels a strange connection to the vastness of it. The dark, unknowable endlessness of it all.

Thoughts of his brother, of his son, vanish as Jamie looks down into the sand-swirled water, alive with microscopic organisms and particles of everything that lies dead at the bottom dancing in the current.

Jamie cups his hands together, scoops up a handful of water and drinks it. He scoops another handful, and another. Finally, he lowers his whole face into the water and swallows as much as he can. The stomach spasms don't hurt as much anymore, but he can't get enough water.

Keeping his head in the ocean, Jamie lies down, stretches out, and lets his body drift in the current. Feeling, for however long he can, part of a system so much bigger than himself. An organism in the ocean on a planet in a galaxy, in a universe made of space, time, fire, and darkness.

He drifts.

SOMETHING NEW

To: Dr. Anderson Packett
Re: An Investigation into Unknown Species

Dr. Packett,

Following up on my previous email regarding the number of unusual species being netted by local fishing vessels.

At first, this seemed to be an isolated event. As you may recall, we only received a couple reports of unidentified species being caught off the coast. However, within the last two weeks, these reports have increased to the point of, in the words of one captain, "happening every time we bring a net in."

Furthermore, we have received multiple reports on the aggressive nature of these animals. Several vessels have stated that these unknown fish appear to be from deep water, based on their appearance, defense mechanisms, and aggression. One captain reported that he netted a number of fish he didn't recognize, and that when brought on board, these fish proceeded to attack and kill most of his catch. Thankfully, he was able to preserve a sample of two of the unknown species and bring them to the university for study.

The samples brought in were both deceased, but it was easy to understand how they could easily maim and kill so many fish within a few minutes. The teeth, as I mentioned in my previous letter, are incredibly sharp, but also fragile. They tend to fracture at the halfway point, leaving the other end embedded within the prey. When broken off, the remaining tooth becomes even more jagged, meaning the prey is ripped up, rather than just killed and eaten. According to the captain that brought in these samples, the killing seemed to be the point. Meaning, he did not witness any of the unknown species eating what they'd killed.

I cannot stress to you enough how concerning these reports are. The samples I studied are both highly unusual and violent creatures with similarities to several deep sea, and shallow water creatures. For example, one fish that measured nearly four feet in length, shared characteristics of both an eel and a shark, with the teeth and eyes of an angler. That description sounds unlikely, but please believe me when I tell you this is a highly developed predatory species.

Now, this may give you some pause, but please hear me out. The two fish I inspected, were both different species (the other appeared to be something akin to a yellowfin tuna, with some kind of parasitic worm attached to its intestines that used the mouth of the fish as its catch) but they both shared certain visual qualities one would not expect to see. They looked, externally, anyway, to be of a similar design.

I'm hoping that you will call me immediately to discuss what steps need to be taken, but I want to give you one additional piece of information.

A friend of mine who scuba dives frequently around Ahua Reef asked me to join him yesterday and give my opinion on something he found. We went diving and he took me approximately a quarter mile out, to where the reef begins to thin. Just beyond this point, on the ocean floor, we discovered a type of coral I have not seen before. Ranging from bright orange to red in color, this coral appears similar to honeycomb coral, but differentiates in some pretty substantial ways. Firstly, there is very little variation within each comb. Meaning, all combs appear to be of equal size and shape, which is highly unusual, as you know. It gives the coral the appearance of something "manufactured." Secondly, it is also incredibly sharp. I touched it once to get a feel of its consistency, and my rubber gloves came away shredded.

Upon further observation, this "blood coral" as my friend so elegantly calls it, is growing into and taking over the existing coral reef. A bit farther out, he showed me where the Ahua Reef ended previously, and it is now covered with blood coral. As far as I can tell, it grows much faster than its native counterparts, and I estimate that it won't be long until it is the primary coral species within the reef.

While we were diving, we also witnessed a number of varying fishes which closely resembled the reports I've received from fishermen. And I saw one fish, briefly, that matched the eel-like creature I'd analyzed at the university.

I need to make sure I am explicitly clear on a point. As we dove, I saw and photographed various flora that I cannot identify, along with a variety of fish species. It is my assessment that, through some shift within the oceanic atmosphere, we are witnessing a host of new species encroaching upon the ecosystem we know and understand.

Dr. Packett, I believe these, as of now, "unknown" species are actively creating their own ecosystem which exists independently of, and through the destruction of - our current one. This is an urgent matter which requires all available resources immediately. It is my recommendation that we alert the federal government of our findings as soon as possible, so that we can begin to understand what's happening off our coast. I have reached out to several colleagues in Australia, Japan, and California to see if this phenomenon is isolated to our islands or occurring globally. Either way, we need to act with ruthless efficiency before we lose a world we understand to a new and unknown world that is rising up beneath us.

I eagerly await your reply.

Dr. Naomi Kapur
Department of Marine Biology
University of Hawaii

ACKNOWLEDGMENTS

Rae Lyn, for a life so much better than I deserve, for a love deeper than an ocean.

Liam, for your kindness, bravery, and perseverance.

Quinn, for your creativity, energy, imagination, and strength.

Jim Wright, for teaching me when to hold on and when to let go.

Maureen Wright, for showing me what courage and compassion look like in action.

Mom and Dad Jones, for love and support.

Ryan Mills, for the incredible artwork and creative input.

Austrian Spencer, for editing this book with skill and grace.

Phil Haagensen, for invaluable friendship and insight.

Brennan LaFaro, for the "constant conversation" on art and life.

Ross Jeffery, for endless support and encouragement.

Philip Fracassi, for helping me navigate uncharted waters.

Elizabeth Copps, for advice, encouragement, and wisdom.

Andrew Robert, for believing in this book and working so hard to give it a good home.

A NOTE FROM DARKLIT PRESS

All of us at DarkLit Press want to thank you for taking the time to read this book. Words cannot describe how grateful we are knowing that you spent your valuable time and hard-earned money on our publication. We appreciate any and all feedback from readers, good or bad. Reviews are extremely helpful for indie authors and small businesses (like us). We hope you'll take a moment to share your thoughts on Goodreads and/or BookBub.

You can also find us on all the major social platforms, including Facebook, Instagram, and Twitter. Our horror community newsletter comes jam-packed with giveaways, free or deeply discounted books, deals on apparel, writing opportunities, and insights from genre enthusiasts.

VISIT OUR LITTLE-FREE-LIBRARY OF HORRORS!

ABOUT THE AUTHOR

Tyler Jones is the author of *Criterium, The Dark Side of the Room, Almost Ruth,* the story collection *Burn the Plans* (one of Esquire magazine's Best Horror Books of 2022), and *Midas.* His work has appeared in multiple anthologies including *Burnt Tongues* (edited by Chuck Palahniuk), *Campfire Macabre, Paranormal Contact,* and in *Cemetery Dance, LitReactor,* and *The NoSleep Podcast.* He lives in Portland, Oregon.

www.tylerjones.net

CONTENT WARNINGS

Graphic violence

Blood and gore

Depictions of abuse